THE DOUBLE M MAN

Mike M'Call arrived in West Africa to sell guns. He had already arranged an initial contract with the Federal Government of Nigeria, but now the country was torn by an unexpected revolt. The situation became further complicated by an approach from the rebels, and M'Call's philosophy of non-involvement was severely jeopardised by a girl with a problem. He ended up with his life balanced with that of pretty Virginia West on a razor's edge.

Books by Charles Leader
in the Linford Mystery Library:

A WREATH OF POPPIES
A WREATH FOR MISS WONG
A WREATH FROM BANGKOK
A WREATH OF CHERRY BLOSSOM

CHARLES LEADER

THE DOUBLE M MAN

Complete and Unabridged

LINFORD
Leicester

First published in Great Britain

First Linford Edition
published 1996

British Library CIP Data

Leader, Charles, *1938* –
    The double M man.—Large print ed.—
Linford mystery library
1. English fiction—20th century
2. Large type books
I. Title
823.9'14 [F]

ISBN 0–7089–7940–8

Published by
F. A. Thorpe (Publishing) Ltd.
Anstey, Leicestershire

Set by Words & Graphics Ltd.
Anstey, Leicestershire
Printed and bound in Great Britain by
T. J. Press (Padstow) Ltd., Padstow, Cornwall

This book is printed on acid-free paper

1

Strong Man

The card read:

> Major Michael M'Call
> Munitions Manipulator
> Trans-Global Arms Co.

IT was my card, but it wasn't strictly accurate. I served fifteen years in the Royal Marines but I never made higher than sergeant. I wasn't officer class. Trans-Global knew that, but most of our customers were Generals, of one sort or another, and so the firm turned a blind eye to the fact that I had upranked myself on my calling card. Generals could be contemptuous of talking business with mere sergeants, even though that sergeant knew more about arms than most of them knew about their own mothers. So it was a business necessity to appear a near-equal, and Major fitted just right. It was high enough to carry a little weight, and low enough to leave room for those comforting feelings of seniority so vital to a new General's ego. In an age of political upheavals and emerging nations few Generals lasted for long, and those that were around at any given time could all be considered new.

This particular General who was now holding my card in his carefully manicured black hands was one Daniel Makefa, for the present the most powerful man in Nigeria. He sat behind a colossal oak desk that was just a little smaller than the bridge of the Q4. The desk helped the impression of a man steering a nation, as though it had been built with forethought for the day when political chaos opened the door for a military takeover. That

2

sort of thing was not exactly difficult to foresee, it was happening everywhere and military takeovers were an ugly rash on the world map. Nigeria's turn had come two days previously with a sharp rebellion by the usual clique of young army officers.

The revolt had been only a partial success. The mutineers had massacred a choice selection of their senior officers, a few tribal chiefs and an assortment of politicians. They had also taken over the northern towns of Kano and Kaduna, and stage-managed the kidnapping of Nigeria's Federal Premier, Sir Stanley Okuwa. On the other side of the coin the main rebellion in the south had been quickly and savagely crushed by the loyal Federal Army under Makefa's command. Lagos, the Federal capital, was now under firm military control, and the badly shaken Government, headless without Okuwa, had temporarily handed over its powers to martial law. On the road in from the airport a few hours earlier I had noticed barbed-wire barricades going up around the city, and the streets swarmed with heavily armed patrols of Federal troops, either keeping the nervous civil population on the move or guarding the Government buildings and key points. General Daniel Makefa had emerged as the latest Johnny Strongman in this part of Africa, and here in Lagos he was King.

I watched him as he studied my calling card and made a preliminary assessment. It's a good aid to business if you can calculate the strengths and weaknesses of your opponents, and I had worked out a little mental routine of my own to help with the process. I simply visualised a questionnaire file card, filled in the blank spaces in my mind, and then slotted it back into the archives of my memory. By asking myself definite questions I had to arrive at definite answers, and although they were not always right they were a guide that could be modified as I went along.

In Makefa's case the file was not too difficult. Under the general background heading I could note that he was an educated Nigerian from one of the Yoruba tribes of the western region. He had received his military schooling at Sandhurst and then returned to a fast-climbing career in the Federal army. He was now a General at thirty-eight, although he had done nothing spectacular to warrant it. Somewhere he undoubtedly had influence. He had no wife but there were vague rumours of a mistress.

The remaining spaces on my mental card were headed Physical, Mental, Emotional, and Weaknesses, and I could answer them all without too many doubts. Physically Makefa was muscular and heavily built, a hard and forceful type of man. Mentally shrewd, and a careful planner who obviously timed his moves. Emotionally he would be as stable an any African with burning fires of ambition. Weaknesses there were none evident, but I entered ambition and mistress and added a ringed query to each.

My final summing up was that he probably preferred Okuwa dead, despite his show of loyalty; and that like so many of his kind he was destined to a brief reign of glory, a violent end, and a dictator's obituary.

He fingered my calling card for several seconds, and then placed it exactly in the centre of his spotless white blotter, as though it was an object to be framed and treasured. Then he looked across the desk and pretended that there wasn't such a vast gulf between us after all, smiling at me as though he had found his long-lost brother. Perhaps the fact that I represented fifty armoured scout cars of a reliable British make, plus a shipment of ten thousand brand-new Belgian F.A.L. rifles, had some small influence on the warmth of his welcome. It's also possible that I'm just a cynical lout with no real sensitivity. Anyway, he smiled.

"Major M'Call, I am very pleased to make your acquaintance, even at such a busy time as this. But I understood that you had completed your business with our Government and returned to London. What exactly is the purpose of your return visit?"

He stressed the word return, and I guessed that underneath that loving smile he was just a little bit worried. Perhaps he had reason to be.

I said calmly, "I'm still concerned with the arms shipment which Trans-Global is supplying for the Federal Army. My company isn't exactly happy with the abrupt change in the political situation here in Nigeria, and especially with the disappearance of Sir Stanley Okuwa. Nothing has been seen or heard of the Premier since he was kidnapped, and before we can be sure of our own position we have to know whether he is alive or dead. I'm hoping that you can throw some positive light on to his fate."

Makefa's smile began to evaporate.

He gave me a fixed stare and seemed to decide that I wasn't his long-lost brother. He said slowly,

"I do not think that I understand you. Everything that is known has already been reported in the international press. The Premier was giving a small garden party here in Lagos when his home was attacked. He has a house on the mainland overlooking the lagoon. The assault was one of a dozen simultaneous moves by the rebel elements. The servants at the house were murdered and so were all of Sir Stanley's guests, including chiefs Seletso and Kalewa who were two of his foremost supporters in the Federal Government. When my troops arrived there was no sign of Sir Stanley himself, and it can only be assumed that the rebels took him away alive. We think that he was taken north, probably by a waiting plane, and probably to either Kano or Kaduna which are still in rebel hands. This was two days since and we have heard nothing more. All this you must already know from the newspapers, and it is all that I can tell you."

I nodded gently. "I do know that much. But it isn't always expedient to tell all the facts to the newspapers, or to release all the facts at the same time. It is often more wise to psychologically prepare the general public for any really bad news, and of course new facts are emerging all the time. I'm just hoping that you can bring me up to date on any late developments."

"There are no late developments." Makefa spoke stiffly and now the smile had wholly vanished. He repeated, "I know nothing more than has already been released to the press. Naturally reports are still coming in from different parts of the country, but they are garbled and conflicting. They have to be corroborated before any of them can be accepted as fact, and for the moment there is much confusion and no definite news of the Premier. We can only hope that he is still alive."

"Then what is your personal opinion? It's been assumed that the rebels wanted Sir Stanley as a hostage, to use as a bargaining point to pressure your Government. But so far that hasn't happened. Does that mean that he is dead, or is there any other reason that they might have for keeping him alive?"

"Perhaps they hope to force the Premier into accepting some of their demands, rather than use him as a lever to move the Government." Makefa's tone was cold, but he did not forget to use a theatrical shrug as he added. "I cannot know. As yet it is unclear what their demands are."

I let that pass. The rebels had made a radio broadcast claiming that they had acted to stop rot and corruption in the Government, but I knew what Makefa's answer would be to that. First a vigorous denial that there was anything wrong with the present system, and second an earnest assertion that revolutionaries anywhere usually created their reasons as an afterthought, their basic desire being power. I would have agreed that power-lust was the prime self-destructive flaw in the collective human psyche. Those that had power were fighting to hang on to it, and those that hadn't were fighting to obtain it, while those who could were making money while the blood flowed. In any war or revolution it was only the details and the degrees of honesty and villainy that varied. In short I had as much faith in the sincerity of any group of rebels as I had in the incorruptibility of any Government. I could have agreed and disagreed with Makefa in equal proportions.

However, I was not here in the role of judge or jury. I was here simply as an arms salesman, which was normally a whole lot easier. There was no need to touch the deeper issues of the subject, and Makefa already had another subject on his mind. He said pointedly,

"I am still at a loss to understand

the reason for your visit, Major. The events of the past few days have created a serious crisis for Nigeria, but I cannot see why they should have a sudden personal interest for you, or for your company. Surely these events cannot affect a business agreement that has already been signed between Trans-Global Arms and my Government."

"But I'm afraid that they can." I tried to sound apologetic, as though this wasn't my fault and I didn't really want to be here. Which was true except that I didn't feel particularly apologetic about it. I went on.

"The British Government is very careful and moralistic in regard to where and to whom it allows arms to be sold. And Trans-Global, being a British firm, is subject to British restrictions and regulations."

"But you already have the necessary clearance papers!" Makefa interrupted sharply.

I nodded but had to explain. "Those papers were issued when we were dealing with a stable Federal Government, part of the British Commonwealth, and headed by Sir Stanley Okuwa, who was regarded in London as one of Britain's staunchest friends among the reshaped nations of Africa. Now that is all changed. Nigeria is divided between rebels to the north and the army here in the south. Nobody knows whether a freely elected Government can emerge again or whether a military dictatorship will continue. Nobody can be sure whether Nigeria will remain in the Commonwealth. Nobody can be sure whether Sir Stanley is alive or dead. And if he is dead then it is doubtful whether anyone else can weld the hostile political parties together into any sort of harmony. Nigeria's future is very uncertain indeed, with the strong possibility of a civil war. No one wants to throw fuel on the flames, and you must admit that the British Government has good cause to review the situation. That's why Trans-Global have been asked to hold back that arms shipment."

"But the agreement has already been signed!"

"By Sir Stanley Okuwa," I reminded him gently. "Who is now missing, and possibly dead."

Makefa snapped angrily. "The money has been paid!"

I shook my head slowly. "I'm sorry, General, but there you have been misled. It was a cash on delivery contract."

Makefa glared at me across the huge desk. Without realising the fact he had picked up my calling card from his white blotter and his right fist was crushing it into a dry pulp. Apart from that his self control was pretty good. He said coldly.

"Major M'Call, that arms contract was signed between your company and the Federal Government of Nigeria. In the absence of the Premier I now represent that Government with the full approval and authority of the cabinet of ministers. Neither the Trans-Global Arms Company nor the British Government have any right to withhold that arms shipment."

I nodded in agreement. I had explained the position and now I had to soothe him and make him more amenable to my way of thinking.

"Privately I'm inclined to sympathise with your viewpoint. This kind of last minute dithering doesn't get anyone anywhere. It merely annoys and frustrates everybody concerned. Unfortunately the British Government has decided to dither, and my company has to abide by their decision. There's nothing that can be done until the situation becomes more precise. That's why Trans-Global have sent me back to Nigeria; to explain the delay, and to try and obtain a clearer picture of what is happening."

I paused, because I was now about to skate on rather thin ice, and then said delicately, "It would help if I could make a positive report that Sir Stanley was dead. Once that mystery is resolved, one way or another, it will help the British Government to make up their minds."

That was as near as I dared get to being frank. It meant that if Okuwa was still alive then he might not be conformant with his cabinet's decision to hand over the reins of power to the army, especially if Makefa, having tasted power, proved reluctant to hand them back. That was Britain's worry. If Okuwa was dead and Makefa the sole legitimate heir apparent then the arms shipment would be released. If Okuwa was alive and he and Makefa could work together in harmony then the arms shipment would be released. The big fear was that Okuwa was alive and that a disintegrating Nigeria would be even further split by a new power struggle between the Premier and the General.

I could only hope that Makefa could read all that from the little that I had said aloud, for it would have been tactless to spell it all out in detail.

It would have been casting doubts upon his much-applauded integrity and loyalty, and no doubt regarded as an insult. He stared at me hard, as though he was trying to understand, and then said curtly,

"Major M'Call, I can assure you that I am as anxious as you to learn the truth surrounding our Premier — and as ignorant of it."

I spread my hands regretfully. "Then I'm sorry, General, the arms shipment will have to wait until we both learn a little more. Trans-Global can do nothing until we have more facts with which to approach the British Government."

Makefa dropped the mangled card that bore my name. Then he picked up a pencil, glowered at it, and snapped it in two. For good measure he snapped the two halves into four, and then he looked up again.

"Where are the arms now?"

"They've got as far as Sierra Leone. They're aboard the *African Rose* which is docked at Freetown. That's only three day's sail from here, but she won't leave until she gets government permission to deliver those arms. It's also possible that she might by-pass Lagos until her homeward voyage from South Africa. I doubt if she can afford to sit around in port for very long."

"For the ship to go to South Africa first and then call back here would take weeks." Makefa's hands were searching for more pencils to break but didn't find one. His eyes were glaring into my face. "Do you not realise that Nigeria is still facing an armed rebellion in the north. I need those armoured cars and I need those rifles. I cannot put down a mutiny without them!"

I spread my hands again. "I'm sorry. I'll help you when I can. But there's nothing that I can do until the situation clarifies."

Makefa stilled his hands and rested his arms heavily on the desk. He said ominously,

"If Trans-Global cannot honour our

contract then perhaps it will be more simple to scrap that contract altogether. There are other sources of arms and ammunition."

He was bluffing and he knew it. I said bluntly,

"Any other British firm would be subject to the same restrictions as Trans-Global, and the Americans would be unlikely to contravene British policy. The only real alternative sources of supply are the Russians and the Chinese, and they won't help you. Despite our present difficulties you are still the chief spokesman for the lawful Government of a Commonwealth nation friendly to the West. You know as well as I that if the Communist bloc feeds arms into Nigeria then they will only feed them to the rebels. That's the way the world works."

"If Britain appreciates that fact then she should release those arms that are already under contract to me."

"They will be released," I said placatingly. "I'm sure that this hold-up

19

can only be temporary. At the moment some Nervous Nellie in Whitehall is playing safe and sitting tight, but I can guarantee that Trans-Global's managing director in London will be doing everything that is possible at that end. When we get some definite news of the Premier's whereabouts, that will be the deciding factor. His fate can't remain a total mystery for much longer. If the rebels have him alive and intend to use him then they must make an announcement soon. If we don't hear anything then we must assume that he's dead and work from there."

"And meanwhile the rebels strengthen their grip on the northern regions — while I sit here and wait for arms that are deliberately held-up in Freetown."

"I can only say again that I'm sorry."

"You are sorry. I am sorry too! And I am beginning to think that there must be more alternative sources of supply than the Russians and the Chinese. What about the French, or the West Germans? And in America there are many private dealers who can sometimes cut corners around official policy."

"Those are all possibles," I conceded. "But a deal of this kind takes time to arrange. It can take weeks, sometimes months. Our shipment is only three days away, and we'll deliver fast as soon as we can get the necessary clearance."

"But you have already had the necessary official clearance!"

"And we've been officially asked to hold back on delivery until London has had time to review the new shape of Nigeria. Legally we could go ahead, but that isn't going to help us to gain Government approval for future contracts. Trans-Global is in an awkward position, we need a licence to deal in arms, and so we have to let the Government dictate."

"It is most irregular." Makefa was now frustrated as well as angry. "I shall protest to the British High Commission here in Lagos, and I shall instruct the Nigerian High Commission in London to protest directly and strongly to your Government in London."

"That does seem the best course of action." I approved because it was much better than protesting to me. I was just the unlucky dogsbody in the middle. "I can promise you that Trans-Global will honour our contract as soon as possible. And personally I shall be as relieved as you to get the whole matter finally settled."

Makefa's black face was grim and thunderous, but he knew that he had no real choice. He could only make his protests and then wait until some desk-bound warrior in Whitehall decided to say yea or nay. His hands still failed to find a pencil, but they did locate a wooden ruler that lay beside his blotter. He gripped it between both fists and savagely broke it.

2

Golden Girl

THE interview lasted another ten minutes but it carried neither of us any further. At the end we parted without shaking hands and I promised to keep in touch. Makefa made sure that I couldn't welsh on my promises by providing me with a staff car and a young army lieutenant as a guide-chauffeur.

Lieutenant Kamau was handsome and athletic looking, and I doubted whether he was much more than twenty-five years old. I didn't doubt that he went down big with the native girls, and perhaps a few white girls as well. When we were introduced he eyed me almost as dubiously as I eyed him, but the General was watching so we shook hands and pretended that we liked each other. The staff car was a Jaguar Mark II saloon, and with Kamau driving we left Army H.Q. and headed back into Lagos. The Lieutenant was sociable and polite, but I was broody and so we didn't form any immediate friendship.

I noticed that there were more barricades going up, and there were droves of military vehicles flying to and fro, apparently with the sole intention of seeing who could create the thickest dust cloud. There were steel-helmeted soldiers lurking behind every coconut palm, and it seemed as though every flowering shrub or clump of trailing bougainvillaea in the gardens facing the road had suddenly sprouted an ugly blossom of black gun barrels. There was a heavy guard on the bridge that linked Lagos Island to the mainland, and on the whole it looked at though Makefa seriously expected the rebel forces to start dropping from the sky in their millions. The fact that the rebels would probably have to stretch their resources to air-lift a squad of boy scouts hadn't prevented him from taking all possible precautions.

The subject of precautions made me wonder whether I should have told Makefa quite bluntly that I didn't need his watchdog. I wasn't exactly a six-foot-plus superman, but at five-foot-ten-and-a-half I was big enough to take care of myself against most people. I was at least an inch bigger than Kamau anyway.

However, once again it wasn't difficult to predict what the General's answer would have been. He would have replied with a sincere and touching concern for my personal safety in his unsettled city. If I had brushed that aside he would have argued a little, and then wondered why I expressly did *not* want a bodyguard. What did I wish to do in Lagos that I had to do alone? Where did I wish to go where it would be inconvenient for my guide to accompany me I have never yet met an Asian or an African who could fully understand an Englishman's peculiar desire to maintain his reserve and his privacy. All kinds of dark suspicions would have been aroused in the General's mind, and so it was easier to accept my guide-chauffeur without protest. I had learned how hopeless it was to openly protest in the Middle East, and other parts of Africa, and I knew all about the complications that could ensue.

Kamau stopped the car in the forecourt outside the Ambassadors Hotel, a brand-new, four-square block of glass and gleaming white concrete that only expense-account travellers could afford, plus of course the rare millionaire. He turned towards me and smiled, showing a set of perfect white teeth. He obviously used his toothbrush three times a day, and somehow that made me feel inferior because I only brushed twice. He said politely,

"Here is your hotel, Major M'Call. What time will you be requiring the car this afternoon?"

I put on my best pondering expression. The trick here was to be casual and pretend that I didn't know that he was meant to be my watchdog. If I was vague enough then he had to keep his distance and risk losing me, or make himself obvious and risk offending me, and his orders were almost certainly to do neither. It was much easier to befuddle a lieutenant than to argue with a general, especially now that I had the theoretical advantage of rank.

I said at last, "I don't think that I shall be needing the car at all. I only arrived in Lagos this morning, and then went directly to see the General. I haven't yet had time to unpack. Also I find the heat tiresome — I'll probably rest through this afternoon."

"This evening then?" Kamau tried to sound as though it wasn't important to him either. "Perhaps you will want to go out to a restaurant, or a night club?"

I smiled. "Perhaps, but I've no definite plans. I'll probably eat here at the hotel. You'd best call me tomorrow. I might need you then to take me back to Army H.Q. I have to keep in close touch with the General."

It was a careless dismissal. Kamau wasn't too happy about it, but he couldn't let it show. I got out of the car and he got out too, standing to attention and saluting smartly as I moved off into the hotel. I gave him another smile and a parting wave and then didn't look back. I knew he'd stick around but at least he wouldn't be treading on my heels.

The foyer of the Ambassadors was almost as grand as the interior of a Greek temple. There were doric columns, marble floors, and even a small fountain where a green marble mermaid attempted to hold a bubbling cascade of cool water in her cupped hands. It was air-conditioned and nobody sweated, a shadowed relief after the blaze of the West African sun outside. I gave one of my rare displays of will-power and avoided the tempting glitter of the lounge bar leading off to the right. Instead I picked up my key at the desk and allowed a bright-eyed page boy in a red fez and a blue uniform to whisk me up to the third floor in a lift that was obviously his pride and joy.

I had a room that was fit for a duke, and I had long since got over feeling self-conscious in a room like that. Trans-Global could afford not to be stingey over their expense accounts, and I didn't have to tell anyone that my humble origins led back to the sergeants' Mess. Once inside I stripped naked and marched into the bathroom for a cold shower. The water really was cold, not just tepid, and I came out with a towel around my waist feeling fit for anything.

The next job was to fix myself a drink; a medium-sized measure of Seagram's V.O., a small bottle of dry ginger ale and several large chunks of ice. As the day wore on I usually cut down on the ginger ale and ice, but here in the hot lands of perpetual thirst it was best not to start on the real drinks too early. I wandered out towards the balcony window, not too close because I was still wearing only the towel, and looking out towards the lagoon I let the mellow Seagram's roll around my tongue and pondered.

It was a damned nuisance that I had to come back here over a deal that should have been all sewn-up. Selling arms was one thing, it was a job I knew backwards, but these political complications that set in afterwards were not my line of business at all. It was a great pity that the Nigerians could not have held back their revolution until after the *African Rose* had docked and unloaded her cargo, then it would have been too late for the unknown in the Foreign Office at Whitehall to have inserted a meddling finger. It was practically certain that the arms would eventually be released to Makefa anyway, which made these last-minute jitters of conscience and delaying tactics doubly annoying. Everybody's feathers got ruffled up the wrong way and in the final analysis no useful purpose was served. My chief complaint was that I had been landed in the middle. It was obvious that Makefa wasn't going to tell me anything until he was ready to tell the rest of the world, and in the meantime I had to listen to his threats and protests.

I wondered for a moment whether Sir Stanley Okuwa would turn up alive. Personally I hoped that he would. I had seen a lot of Okuwa on my earlier trips to Lagos when we had discussed the terms of the present arms contract, and I had both liked and respected him. I'm not exactly an impressionable man, and I have extra doubts over politicians and national leaders, so for me to have been impressed means that Okuwa was far above the average. If he was dead it was not only a complication for Trans-Global, it was a tragedy for Nigeria, and perhaps the whole of Africa.

Knowing that man's inhumanity to man was matched only by his blind

31

stupidity, I had the horrible fear that Okuwa probably was dead.

I finished my drink and my thinking, for both could be overdone in the heat. Then I went back into the bedroom to the telephone. I called room service and asked them to send up a plate of chicken sandwiches and a bottle of cold lager, because my stomach was making comments about the long lull since breakfast on the plane. While I had the receiver in my hand I also called up the hotel desk and asked them to arrange a call through to Trans-Global in London. I would have to report and tell them that they had wasted their time in sending me out here. I knew no more at this end than they knew at theirs.

I put the phone down and then opened up my suitcase and my travelling wardrobe bag which contained two spare suits and four white shirts neatly arranged on hangers, for I had been telling the truth when I told Kamau that I had not yet had time to unpack.

I had also been telling the truth when I said that it was too hot to wander abroad, and decided that after I had tidied up and eaten then the best way to spend the afternoon would be to relax on the bed until it became cool.

★ ★ ★

It was eight o'clock in the evening before I ventured forth from the hotel. My call to London had been put through at six and that had left a sour taste in my mouth. Murchison, Trans-Global's managing director, had been peevish because I had nothing new and helpful to tell him, and more peevish because I had wasted a long-distance call on a negative report. He would also have been peevish if I hadn't called and had left him guessing. It was one of those days when I just couldn't win, and I decided to chuck it all for a few hours and go out on the town.

I put on a light-weight, dark grey suit, with a fresh white nylon shirt. It was now cool enough to make a tie bearable so I selected the blue and grey silk that managed to look tasteful and old-schoolish without exactly representing anything. Being conceited I also wore the heavy gold cufflinks with the double M insignia in black scroll. The initials stood for Munitions Manipulator or Mike M'Call, it didn't really matter which way you looked at them. I did have one ex-flame who claimed that they stood for moral-laxity and mauling, but I never did figure exactly what she meant.

I left the Ambassadors and was quite prepared to walk, but I didn't make it across the forecourt before the black Jaguar saloon was pulling up beside me. Lieutenant Kamau was smiling through the open window as though he was delighted that pure chance had brought him to the spot just in time to be of service.

"Major M'Call, I thought that perhaps you would change your mind and seek some entertainment, and it would be inhospitable if there were no host to show you around our fine city."

I smiled too, but it was mostly at myself. I should have known better than to think that I had got rid of him. I walked around the car to get into the passenger seat beside him and said blandly,

"I did change my mind about eating at the hotel. It was lucky that you were passing."

Kamau nodded. He had changed out of his lieutenant's uniform and was now wearing a more sociable suit, white shirt and tie. He looked at me and asked,

"Where would you like to go?"

I shrugged. "A night club of some kind. I'd like a good meal, a bottle of wine, and perhaps some cabaret to watch. My tastes are simple."

"Then we will go to the 'Golden Bamboo'."

"No, too bright and noisy." I couldn't let him have it all his own way. "Let's try the 'Blue Oasis'."

"As you wish."

Kamau didn't really care where we went as long as we went together. That was what the General had ordered.

The 'Blue Oasis' was one of those dark, moody places that exist in every capital city. The blue-shaded lights were always dim, and the singer always sang sad love songs that made the young lovers in the corners doubly glad that they still had each other. I decided after we had arrived that tonight I would have preferred the more brash and exotic 'Golden Bamboo' but just for the hell of it I had voted exactly opposite to Kamau. Now I was stuck with the place.

I allowed Kamau to order. I had already decided that if he wanted to play host he could pick up the bill afterwards, so it seemed reasonable to let him choose the food. While we waited I idled over a large Seagram's V.O. with a limited amount of ginger ale and ice, listening to the quiet music from the three-piece band in blue-ruffed shirts who occupied the small stage. The cabaret came later. Kamau drank lager and made an effort at friendly conversation.

There was no point in bearing a grudge so I helped him along. We both relaxed and the evening passed smoothly. The food arrived and Kamau explained that it was a West African fish curry, the speciality of the house. I didn't like the sound of it or the look of it, but it tasted excellent. Kamau was pleased. A chocolate-brown Negress in a slinky red dress appeared to join the three musicians and sang softly into the microphone. A few couples danced slowly. Kamau's conversation had lapsed while we ate, and then I saw the golden girl.

There was no other word to describe her. She wore a gold-coloured sheath dress with gloves and handbag to match. Her bare arms were tanned a beautiful sun-golden brown, while her hair was the same smooth bronze colour of the mellowed Canadian whisky in my glass. She sat alone, a few tables away, and I had to think for a moment and then decided that I must have passed her this morning in the foyer at the Ambassadors. She glanced towards me and then I had to stop staring.

I wondered why a white girl as lovely as that should be unaccompanied. In a place like this it didn't seem right. I was tempted to try and do something about it, and then found myself resenting Kamau again. This time I couldn't let it show because it wasn't his fault.

For the next half-hour my attention was split three ways; partly with listening to Kamau, partly with both listening to and watching the cabaret, and partly with wondering about the girl in the golden dress. I had the strange feeling that she might have followed me here, and that she might have approached me if I had been alone. The idea persisted until I stamped it down as mere wishful thinking. I looked several times in her direction, but she was watching the cabaret. She was receiving hopeful male glances from other corners too, but she answered none of them.

Finally a young Negro got up and went over to her table. The schoolboy inside me sat up and hoped for a scene in which I could star as the knight in shining armour, but there wasn't a scene. The girl just shook her head, and made the negative gesture of covering her glass with her hand. The man apologised politely and went back to his table. I felt surprised, because I had honestly thought that the schoolboy inside me had died many, many years ago. Perhaps that was the trouble with the whole world. None of us ever really grew up. I was still examining this unexpected part of my psychology when the girl finished her drink, collected her handbag, and left. She hadn't even eaten, which left me wondering again why she had come.

After that the evening began to drag. I decided anew that I wasn't in the right mood for blue atmosphere and sad songs, and again I was dissatisfied with Kamau's company. I had already fitted the young Nigerian into one of my mental file cards. Like Daniel Makefa he was an educated Yoruba from the west who had done his army training at Sandhurst. The identical general background probably explained why the General had faith in him. Physically he was light but would be fast. Mentally he was intelligent but would lack the judgement of experience. Emotionally he was cheerful but I had already detected a patriotic zeal. He was a firm nationalist. After talking to him throughout the evening I was beginning to like him, but I would not have gambled on his future. He had the courage and conviction of youth, but could so easily be led to an unheroic death on the wrong road.

Having analysed him I found that his talk was beginning to pall. So far we had steered clear of the revolution, politics and the topics of the past few days, but I could sense that he was eager to open them up. Once started he would discuss the whole thing passionately until the early hours and tonight I was tired. Maybe tomorrow I would give him his head and hope to reinforce my own scanty knowledge of the situation, but not tonight. He wouldn't know the answer to the big question anyway, and tonight it was time to go home. The evening hadn't been a roaring success, but I had spent worse and at least we had broken the ice.

I waited until the singer in the red dress had finished her present song, and then suggested that we wound the evening up. It was still early by night club standards but Kamau readily consented. He was playing the perfect host.

We drove back to the Ambassadors Hotel and there he arranged to have the car at my disposal the first thing the following morning. I thanked him for that, and thanked him for a lovely evening, and then bade him good night.

I left him sitting in the car and entered the hotel, but noticed without looking round that he was in no hurry to drive away.

The mermaid in the foyer was still holding up the jet of sparkling water that cascaded back over her green marble face. Apart from that the foyer was empty except for a solitary sentinel behind the reception desk. I circled the fountain, tried hard not to sound like an intruder on the shining floor, and passed close by the entrance to the lounge bar. There were several customers around the glitter of glass and chromium at the far end, and I saw a brief glimpse of a golden dress and a bare and deliciously feminine sun-golden arm. I paused thoughtfully, remembered that Kamau would still be watching me through the wide, plate-glass doors, and then carried on to the lift.

I went up to my room, spent ten minutes by the balcony idly admiring the view of lights across the lagoon, and then descended to the foyer again. There was no sign of the black Jaguar saloon in the forecourt outside, and so I drifted casually into the lounge bar.

The girl was still alone, half-concealed behind a corner, and deep in quiet meditation. I was tempted to go straight to her table, but then changed my mind and went up to the bar. I ordered a Seagram's with a minimum of ginger ale, and then waited for her to notice me.

She did after about two minutes, but it took her several more before she could pluck up the courage to come across. She sat on the red-topped bar stool beside me and there was a short pause.

Finally I looked at her.

She looked at me.

I smiled.

She smiled.

I said calmly, "I have the feeling that you want something, perhaps I can help."

She smiled again. "Somebody told me that you have a reputation with wine and women. I'm a woman, so why not buy me some wine, then we'll see."

3

Moonlight Ride

IT was a good line and she had rehearsed it well. Now that she was close I could see that she had lilac-blue eyes. They fascinated me. I had never seen eyes that wonderful dark shade of blue before. Her cheeks had just the faintest flush of red that was purely natural, and her smile was warm like Spring sunshine. Also she was very young, perhaps nineteen or twenty. She wasn't the worldly-wise, calculating type of female who usually kept such smart opening lines, and that red flush might have indicated some inner embarrassment. However, I decided that they all had to start. Nobody was ever born with experience.

I said in my friendliest fashion, "It's

rather late for wine. Why not try something stronger?"

"All right, I'll have a vodka, with lots of lemon."

I repeated the order to the hovering Negro barman and reflected that in time she would demand lots of vodka with just a taste of lemon. Perhaps I was lucky to get her first. I looked at her again and then there wasn't any doubt about it. I was lucky.

I said, "If you know my reputation then you probably know my name. I'm Mike M'Call. That gives you the advantage over me."

She turned on the spring sunshine again. "Hello, Mike, I'm Virginia West."

"Virginia." I liked that name. It led me straight into the old joke. "I once knew another girl named Virginia. I used to call her Virgin for short — "

"But not for long!"

She had heard it too and she was way ahead of me. This time it wasn't rehearsed and she was rather pleased that she was keeping her end up. But it didn't stop her from adding quickly,

"Don't let it give you any fast ideas."

Her drink arrived. I passed it over and we drank a mutual salute, eyes smiling at each other above the glasses. The barman wore a red jacket and a solemn face and he had seen it all before. He moved discreetly to the other end of the bar. I took out my gold cigarette case with the double M monogram and offered it to her. I said casually,

"The cigarettes are Benson & Hedges, a choice of Silk Cut filter-tipped or Special Menthol. I don't smoke myself, but I always look after my women."

"That's very thoughtful of you." She accepted one of the filter-tips with slender fingers. Lovely fingers. I could already feel them stroking my chest, and perhaps later they would. She couldn't read my thoughts and went on,

"It isn't everyone who panders to

other people's vices."

I put the case away and lit the cigarette for her.

"I believe in live and let live," I explained. "I comply with your vices, perhaps you'll comply with mine."

She looked at me uncertainly.

"Joke," I said quickly. "Perhaps I shouldn't joke until we know each other better. Humour is a matter of taste."

"It can be misunderstood."

"Very true. Let's change the subject. Didn't I see you in the 'Blue Oasis' earlier this evening?"

She nodded. "I was there, but it wasn't the sort of place I should have gone to alone. The men all thought that I was hoping to be picked up. So I had to leave." She paused, innocently. "I remember seeing you there too. You were with a young Nigerian."

"A business acquaintance. He was playing host and showing me some of the night life." I didn't want to talk about Kamau and asked, "Why were

48

you alone? And what are you doing here in Nigeria?"

She only answered the last question. "I've been working here for the past year. Now my job is finished and I'm taking a holiday before I go home. What's your business, Mister M'Call?"

"Mike," I insisted. "I'm going to call you Virginia so you have to call me Mike. And my business isn't really very interesting. I'm just a salesman, and at the moment I'm arranging a contract with the Nigerian Government. It's all rather dull. I prefer talking about you."

We both smiled together, as though we had only just become aware that we were batting the questions back and forth like some kind of double cross-animation. Virginia blushed and I'll swear that it was genuine. Then we each took another sip at our drinks. I broke the pause.

"Are you staying here at the Ambassadors?"

She nodded.

"Then you must be richer than I thought, this place is expensive. Are you a rich man's daughter?"

She laughed. "I sometimes wish that I was. I told you that I was just a working girl. This hotel has got some cheaper rooms at the back, the ones that don't overlook the Lagoon. I'm just doing myself proud for a few days."

"And what was your job when you were working?"

She hesitated. "I was a secretary, but it wasn't really very interesting. Rather dull in fact, and I'd prefer to talk about you."

We laughed, and I said, "Checkmate," and then I bought some more drinks. We talked generally, about the weather and the singer at the 'Blue Oasis'. Then on a sudden impulse I asked,

"Have you ever been swimming by moonlight?"

Virginia looked startled, then recovered her poise. She said cautiously, "Sometimes, why?"

"It was just a thought. It's been a long, hot day, and I've spent the evening in close, smoke-shrouded bars. A swim would be clean and refreshing. There is a moon outside and the beach isn't too far away."

She was wary, but after a moment she said,

"All right, as long as it's only the swim that gets fresh."

"I never make promises," I said blandly. "Do you still want to come?"

At that she smiled once more. "I don't think you can be as dangerous as you make out. I'll take the risk."

It was easier than I had expected. We gave each other the old eyes-salute over the glasses again, drank up, and left.

I went up to my room to collect my swimming trunks and a towel, and spared a few moments for some quiet thought. There was something about Virginia West that wasn't quite true to form. Perhaps it was just that I had never before met a good-time girl with the flushed cheeks of a genuine

51

English Rose, and yet I wasn't quite sure. She was keeping something under the surface, and she asked questions as though she really wanted to know the answers. For the moment she was a mystery, and I was interested.

While I thought I opened up my suitcase, shifted a neat pile of clean socks and underpants, and stared hard at the Browning P-35 in its leather holster. I call the gun my sample and there were some places where I felt safer wearing it. I had never fired it except in practise, but there was always a first time. I hesitated, felt foolish, and then shut the lid of the suitcase. After all, the girl was just a beginner at her trade, and all I had to worry about was the pleasure of teaching her its tricks. I collected my towel and trunks and went back down to the foyer.

Virginia was a true lady, she kept me waiting just three minutes, not too long but just long enough. She had changed into a skirt and blouse and now carried a gay straw beach bag, and she still looked good enough to eat. I put my things in her bag and said,

"I'll call us a taxi. It's not too late to find one."

She looked at me in surprise.

"I thought you would have a car, but if you haven't we can use mine."

"That's fine!" It was certainly a better idea than a taxi. "I only arrived this morning," I explained, "and it's been a busy day. I haven't had time to get organised."

She smiled and we walked out of the hotel. The car was a Ford Corsair that was parked in the far corner of the forecourt, and I noted that it had been hired. She opened it up.

"Would you like to drive, Mike?"

It was a hopeful question, as though she didn't like driving herself, or preferred me to have my hands occupied. I accepted the offer and slid behind the wheel. I leaned across the seat to let her in while she walked around the car, and when she joined me she gave a nervous smile. Some of her confidence had evaporated since we had left the bar, and I tried to put her at ease with some idle chat as I drove away.

We were waved down by the guard detachment on the bridge, but after looking dubiously inside the car the captain in charge let us through. He seemed to think that moonlight swimming was a crazy idea, but it was the sort of thing that the crazy English would do anyway. I drove over to the mainland and then turned west along the coast, looking for a secluded stretch of beach that I had found on one of my previous visits. It was a good ten miles out, but it was a pleasant drive with a million sweet blossom smells carried through the open windows of the car on the night breeze. I remembered the gardens of frangipani, bougainvillaea and eucalyptus trees that I had seen by daylight, although it wasn't so comforting to remember the gun barrels and the lurking troops that were undoubtedly still there.

It crossed my mind quite suddenly

that maybe this night excursion wasn't such a brilliant idea after all, but I would look a fool if I turned back now. The captain at the bridge had been relaxed and unconcerned, and I could only hope that the other Federal troops ringing the island city were all of the same mind. At least it was bright moonlight, and we were very obviously just one harmless private car. Nobody could genuinely mistake us for a hostile convoy.

The thought made me glance into the driving minor, and that was when I realised that we weren't just one car. There was another set of headlights following, and I didn't have to be clairvoyant to guess that they belonged to a black Jaguar saloon. Lieutenant Kamau was on the ball and still doing his pestering duty.

I cursed inwardly, but I could only hope that he would be discreet. Virginia had noticed nothing amiss and sat silently watching the road ahead until I eased the car to a stop beneath a grove of tall coconut palms that overlooked the beach I had in mind. The high fronds threw faintly moving shadows over the empty sands and there was a silver stairway to the moon across the sea. It would have been perfect if we were not being watched. I switched off the engine and said,

"This is it. M'Call's private paradise. You can change in the car while I attempt to hide behind the palm trees."

She smiled. "Call me when you're ready."

I took my trunks and got out of the car. As I closed the door I glanced back along the road towards Lagos but there was no sign of the Jaguar saloon. Kamau must have switched off his lights and braked hard the moment he saw me start to slow down. Perhaps he had done some quick reversing too. There were plenty of patches of black shadow where he might be parked. I settled for another muttered curse, and then went behind the palm trees.

Virginia was ready first. She stepped

out of the car wearing a one-piece white bathing suit that looked pale against her golden skin. She struggled with her bathing cap as I walked to join her, and then she saw the look in my eye, shouted, "Hands off!" and raced down the beach.

I chased her into the sea. The waves were a tingling balm after the heat of the day, and we both came up gasping and laughing. I felt really good and healthy. Virginia looked even better with the water streaming down her shoulders, and we played traditional splashing games before she broke away, shouted, "Race you!" and swam vigorously out to sea. It was all great, unoriginal, clean fun but I've never been able to invent anything else in the water. I swam after her and we kept side by side for some fifteen minutes. Then she looked back and became a little scared by the distance we had put between ourselves and the shore. We took a two-nil vote in favour of a drawn race and then swam all the way back again.

When we could stand she stumbled against me. She was breathing hard but she could still smile. She said unsteadily,

"Phew! I'm puffed."

That was my clue-line and I knocked her legs from under her and lifted her in my arms.

"If you're puffed you can't possibly walk up the beach. I shall have to carry you."

She started to wriggle and protest until I nearly dropped her, and then she gave up and hung on tight as I walked clear of the breaking waves. My knees wobbled as my feet slipped in the soft sand, and I thought that my he-man act was going to end in an ignominious sprawl. With an effort I made it back to the palm trees and dumped her none-too-gently on a towel. She groaned and called me a brute, and then lay back with her eyes closed. I spread another towel and flopped down beside her.

After five minutes she stirred and said,

"Mike, can I have another of those cigarettes you keep for other people's vices?"

"Of course, it's a special service with you in mind."

I had to lean over her to reach my clothes and for a moment I pressed against her. She gave a little jump and I could feel her heart start to flutter, as though this was really unexpected and not planned. I fished my cigarette case and my lighter from my jacket and then withdrew. My lips were close and I brushed them lightly over her bare shoulder. Her skin tasted of salt and sand, but I wasn't complaining. She sat up and said,

"Mike, the cigarette, please."

I sat up too and gave it to her. I gave her a light and watched while she drew in the smoke. She relaxed and looked at me.

"You should try it, Mike. It's not such an awful vice."

"I did once," I admitted. "When I was six years old. I was sick for a whole day and I've never bothered with them since." I smiled and added, "There's the cure for lung cancer that medical science has been seeking for so long. Just give every kid a fag at six and make him smoke it until he throws up."

She laughed, and I began to play walkies with my fingertips along her bare arm. She moved the arm and used one hand to unfasten her bathing cap and take it off. She shook out her hair and it swirled around her neck. The moonlight filtered through the palms and cast our low shadows on the sand, while the breeze and the sea played hushed romantic music. I built a little bridge of sand between her leg and mine, just a playful prelude to walking my fingers over it, and then she looked round behind us and said suddenly,

"Mike, I know it sounds foolish. But do you get the feeling that we're being watched?"

She was more sensitive than I had

imagined, and she was right. I did have that feeling. I sighed inwardly and pretended that it was something new. I looked all around and then said, "I can't see anyone, but if you're nervous I'll scout around for a bit and take a closer look."

She was uncertain, perhaps a bit scared at being left alone, but I squeezed her shoulder and told her to sit tight. I got up and walked through the palms to the road. I could still see nothing but I walked back along the road until at last the black Jaguar took shape in the gloom beneath another clump of palms. I put my head through the open window and said politely,

"Good evening, Lieutenant."

Kamau looked abashed. He said awkwardly,

"Good evening, Major M'Call, I hope you don't think — "

"That you were playing Peeping Tom." I smiled at him reassuringly and shook my head. "No, I didn't think that. After all, we're both soldiers and we both know the meaning of duty. I don't doubt that your orders were to keep a protective eye on me and make sure that I don't get into trouble."

Kamau looked relieved. "Thank you, Major. I am so glad that you understand."

I nodded and then went on. "But as well as being soldiers we're both men of the world. And I think we both know why I would prefer to be alone at the present moment. Quite apart from my tender feelings the young lady doesn't want an audience either. I'm sure we understand each other on that point too."

Kamau nodded unhappily, but I didn't let him interrupt.

"That's fine. Now that we've agreed on that I think we can also agree that I'm not likely to need protecting tonight, nor am I likely to get into trouble. Also I give you my word as an officer that when I leave this beach I shall return direct to the Ambassadors

Hotel and stay there until we meet tomorrow. That means that there is no real need for you to wait up any longer and watch over me."

Kamau tried to look both firm and apologetic at the same time. He started to put his own case but I reached past him to the dashboard and turned on the ignition. I pressed the starter and the engine fired first time. I smiled and said, "Good night, Lieutenant Kamau."

Kamau stopped his protests, hesitated, and then said reluctantly,

"As you wish. Good night, Major M'Call."

I stepped back and waved him away, and after a moment he made a U turn in the road and drove back towards Lagos. I guessed that he would probably stop after a mile or so and wait to trail me home, but at least I had shooed him out of sight and hearing. That had to be enough and I went back to rejoin Virginia.

She was standing up beside the

spread towels and had heard the car drive off. She asked anxiously,

"Who was it?"

I laughed and said, "Just another courting couple. I disturbed them more than they disturbed us. Now they've gone."

She looked relieved and we both sat down. She had finished her cigarette and lay back. I lay back too and our shoulders touched. She was quiet so I began to make the usual idle comments about the beauty of the sky, the moon and the stars, nature's gifts to the poor in which the rich could only share. My foot searched gently for hers across the sand, and then suddenly she asked,

"Mike, do you think there will be civil war in Nigeria?"

The question was so unexpected that I gave it a serious answer.

"It's more than possible. Even if the Federal Government can survive the present revolution it still has the task of holding three basically hostile regions together. The Ibos in the east are particularly incensed about the way the Government is dominated by the north. Martial law might hold the country together for a while, but if Sir Stanley Okuwa is dead then I wouldn't bet much on its immediate future."

She turned to look me in the face and said earnestly,

"Mike, do you care?"

"About Nigeria?" I didn't really understand. "I can't see that it's relevant whether I care or not. I'm not in a position to change anything." I rolled over on to one elbow, closer to her, and added, "Those are funny questions to start shooting at me out of the blue. You should give me some advance warning. And in any case, this is hardly the time or the place to start an abrupt debate on politics."

"Perhaps not, but it was rather important to me."

She sat up and looked toward the sea, so that I couldn't see her face or guess what she was thinking. I reached up and traced my finger around the shoulder straps of her bathing suit but she didn't seem to notice. Instead she had another question.

"What sort of a man are you, Mike? what do you really believe in?"

I said, "That's easy. I believe in good food, sweet wine, and lovely women." As I spoke my fingers had reached the zip of her bathing suit and I carefully pulled it right down.

I'm not sure who was startled the most, she by what I had done, or me by her reaction. She jerked away as though my fingers had become red hot, twisting around on her knees and holding up the top part of her costume. She stared at me and her whole body was suddenly trembling as she said,

"No, Mike, please don't."

That was when it fully sank in that she wasn't just another good-time girl and an easy lay, not even a raw beginner at the game. Instead she was a very frightened and worried little girl, and there had to be another reason why she had approached me tonight.

4

Wrong Play

I SIGHED almost as heavily as the wind creaking the palm fronds, and then wearily I pushed myself up from the sand. Virginia still crouched on her towel, looking scared and making me conscious of how young and clean she was, and how old and dirty I felt. I had guessed that she was acting hard when she had first approached me in the bar, but I hadn't had the sense to look beyond the first explanation that had popped into my mind. Somewhere along the line we had both made a mistake. She was watching my face and I didn't know whether to be gentle or sour. I said at last,

"It's all right, Virgin, you can stop staring at me as though I've just sprouted a blue beard."

I reached down and took her arms and then lifted her up. I turned her round and just as deliberately zipped the bathing costume back into place. She moved round to face me again and her face was flushed with embarrassment. She said awkwardly,

"Mike, I'm sorry. I didn't mean you to think — "

"It doesn't matter, you can tell me later." I gave her a smile that I didn't feel, trying to ease her discomfiture. "Perhaps I should apologise to you, but right now I have the feeling that the evening is over, and it's time we went back. You can change in the car again while I use the palm trees. You'll probably feel happier when we've both got more clothes on."

She looked at me uncertainly and I knew what she was thinking. It made me a little bit angry and I explained the moral facts.

"Look, Virginia, I'm just a normal, disgustingly healthy male animal. When a girl picks me up in a bar and acts as though she wouldn't be impartial to a hot romp on the beach then I'm all in favour of joining in the fun. But at the same time I don't make a habit of raping little girls who are unwilling. You'll be quite safe changing in the car."

She hesitated and then said slowly, "Of course, Mike. I'm sorry." She faltered again then continued wretchedly, "It's all gone wrong. It's all mixed up. You don't understand."

I nodded. "At least we're in agreement on that point. Now go and change in the car."

I picked up her bathing cap and towel from the sand and gave them to her. She hung back another moment, and then turned and walked unhappily to the car. When she reached it she looked back for a moment, and I stopped watching and turned away. I collected my own towel and then moved off into the palm trees where I had left my own clothes. I was dry but I rubbed the sand off my skin and dressed quickly. Then I stood and sourly watched the wasted moonlight painting silver spangles across the sea, giving Virginia plenty of time. When I was sure she would be finished I went back to the Ford Corsair and got in behind the wheel.

It was a silent return drive to Lagos, broken only by a forced halt for the checkpoint on the bridge. The guard had not yet been changed and the captain remembered us. He gave me a knowing grin and then waved us through. It was obvious that I had had a better time in his imagination than I had had upon the beach.

The Ambassadors Hotel loomed above us and I manoeuvred the Corsair back into its original parking space on the forecourt. Virginia had been subdued and downcast since we left the beach, but when I gave her the keys she lifted her head and looked into my face.

"Mike, I really am — "

"Sorry about tonight," I finished for her. "And if you tell me that again I'll scream." I paused and then added, "It's late, but not too late to straighten this out. If you'll come up to my room I'll fix us a drink and we can talk. And I promise to behave myself."

She was very doubtful, but after a moment she nodded her head. We both got out of the car, locked it and then went into the hotel. She looked almost hopefully towards the lounge bar, but it was closed so there was no question of doing our talking in there. We rode up to the third floor in the lift, self-operated at this time of night, and I led the way to my room. I offered her a seat and she sat down, keeping her knees together and holding tightly to her beach bag as though it was possible that I might steal it.

I said, "There isn't any vodka, but I can recommend Seagram's V.O. It's a Canadian bourbon, very nice with dry ginger ale."

She nodded and said, "Please," so I

71

mixed two. A weak one for her and a strong one for me. I took them over and drew up a chair for myself. We both tasted our drinks and I at least felt better. Virginia didn't know where to start so I gave her a little prompting.

"When you came to the 'Blue Oasis' tonight you were following me, isn't that right? You didn't approach me then because I wasn't alone."

She nodded.

I said, "That's fine, if we keep on being honest then we might get somewhere. You followed me to the 'Blue Oasis', but then came back here and waited for me, hoping that I'd get rid of my friend. I did and so you picked me up in the bar. You pretended that you were just free and easy and I was foolish enough to believe that my lucky star was shining double. We both made the wrong play there, but you're still here in my room in the early hours of the morning, alone, unchaperoned, and drinking my whisky. You didn't want fun and games on the beach, so I can be pretty certain that you don't want fun and games in the bedroom. That brings us to the big question; what exactly do you want?"

She said weakly, "I wanted to talk to you."

"Then why didn't you just talk?"

"Because — because I wasn't sure that you were the right man to talk to."

That wasn't very illuminating, but I was trying hard to understand. I said patiently,

"You have a problem, right? You thought that you could bring it to me but you weren't sure. To give yourself time to find out you played me along for a little, pretending to be something that you are not."

"Something like that," she smiled sadly. "But you wanted to — to — "

"To take the game to its natural conclusion a little too soon?"

She smiled a little more bravely, faint traces of the Spring sunshine appearing again.

"That's right, Mike. I didn't mean to be a tease and lure you on, but you were much faster than I expected."

"All right, we'll forget about that." I was in a forgiving mood and I was intrigued. "Tell me about the problem?"

She went quiet again. The sunshine faded and her face was troubled. She toyed with her drink but when she looked up she looked me firmly in the eyes. She said slowly,

"I'm still not sure, Mike. I didn't learn much about you, did I? And this is important."

I closed my eyes and groaned. "A vote of no confidence, that's all I need to complete my evening." I opened my eyes again and asked, "Just as a matter of interest, what made you think that I might have been the right man to approach?"

Her hesitation was the longest yet, and then she said,

"I saw your name in the hotel guest book. Major Michael M'Call, and after it you had added in brackets, ex-Royal Marines. Perhaps it's silly, but my father was also a major in the Marines. Before your time, he's dead now, but — Well, it was just an impulse."

I stared at her. I thought that my ego had already been deflated but now it was being squashed flat. I said helplessly,

"It's impossible! Surely you didn't seriously mistake *me* for the father-figure type?"

"Not exactly." She looked and sounded uncomfortable, and didn't know whether she should look at me or not. "It's just that — What I mean is — "

She was having difficulty so I helped her.

"Perhaps you just thought that there was an officer and a gentleman beneath this rough exterior?" That was still a ridiculous notion, but it was an improvement on the first one. I went on. "I'm sorry to disappoint you, Virginia, but I'm rough all the way to the core." I paused, and then confessed my secret. "I never was an officer in the Marines. I was only a sergeant, but in my present job it's more useful to bill myself as Major."

Now she could look at me. I had rubbed off the last of my glamour and the confession could prove to be a mistake. She stopped being on the defensive and asked bluntly,

"What is your job, Mike?"

I drank from my glass and then set it down on the carpet at my feet. She watched as I reached into my jacket for my wallet, and then I extracted one of my calling cards and gave it to her. She read it, and when she looked up again her lilac-blue eyes were no longer friendly. She said slowly,

"Munitions manipulator?"

I nodded. "A fancy label, but it means arms dealer. I'm handling a sale to the Nigerian Government, fifty armoured scout cars and ten thousand Belgian rifles. The deal should have been closed, but this little rebellion in the north has caused complications."

She was still staring at me, and said coldly,

"If there is going to be more bloodshed then the last thing this country needs is more guns. More guns means more people killed, or can't you see that?"

I didn't agree. "Not necessarily. Violence and killing go hand in hand with man's urge to dominate. You can't stamp that out. If they don't get guns they'll kill each other with bows and arrows, or hack each other to bits with knives and axes. Giving them guns simply means that the same amount of people get killed more quickly, and perhaps more cleanly." I paused and added my philosophical bit. "No gun ever killed a man in anger, not without another man's finger on the trigger. It's men who do the killing."

"But you don't have to help them to kill each other!"

"I'm trying to explain, they don't need any help. The power struggle of man against man has been going on since creation. The first cavemen threw rocks at each other, and then fought with their bare hands. Man would do the same today if he had no other weapons. Progress has only been made in technical and material fields, there's been no progress in man's instincts. He still wants to eat, drink, make love with his women and dominate his neighbours, just as he did two thousand years ago."

"But there's good in man too, as much good as bad. Why can't man understand that we're all the same, and that our neighbours all have the same little hopes and fears that we have ourselves? Why can't we concentrate on the good instead of killing each other over the bad?"

I shrugged. "Perhaps it's nature's way of keeping us all down to a manageable size. All the other animals prey on each other for food and survival. There is no animal more intelligent than man and so man has to prey upon himself to maintain the balance." I was getting deep, but I reached down for my glass, drank thoughtfully and ploughed on.

"You ask why can't we understand that we're all the same, but has it ever occurred to you that we do understand that fact only too well. That's why we all want our country or our side to be top of the heap. We don't trust anybody else up there. We know damn well that they'll be no more just or incorruptible than we would be."

She said bitterly, "Mike, you're a cynic."

I replied sincerely, "Virginia, you're an idealist."

She shook her head. "No, Mike, I don't think that I am. I think that there are three levels of human understanding. The first is idealism, when you're young and have faith in something, either God, or love, or Communism; when you feel that the world can be cured of all its ills if only enough people would work together to that end. The second is cynicism, when you lose your faith and realise that all these things have been tried before and failed; when you realise that life always has been a succession of wars and conflicts and always will be, and that for every man prepared to build there is another who finds it easier to destroy. Then comes the third level, and I don't know what to call it; but it comes when you realise that despite all its faults and evils there is still a vast amount of love and courage and beauty in the world. I think it comes when you learn compassion for the world, when you learn that small ideals can be achieved as long as you don't try to do the impossible."

She paused and then added, "I don't know if I've explained that very well, but I like to think that I've found that third level. And I'm sorry that you've only found the second."

I said wryly, "Maybe I'm in the wrong business. I deal with politicians and generals. I don't find them very loving, or beautiful, or compassionate."

She said with feeling,

"You definitely are in the wrong business."

I didn't want to argue. I was tired and it had been a long day. She watched me while I drank the last of the bourbon in my glass, and then I made an effort to get back on to the original track.

"We seem to have drifted away from the point in question. Now that you know a little more about me, are you going to tell me about your problem or not?"

She looked down at my card again and I knew that I had made another wrong play in being too frank with her. She hadn't been sure whether she could trust me before, and now that she knew that I was only a sergeant who dealt crudely in arms she trusted me even less. She said in a low voice,

"I don't know, Mike. I don't think you're the right man."

I said bluntly, "Then it's time you went home to bed. Sleep on it, and if

81

you change your mind you can always come and see me tomorrow."

She looked relieved that I was prepared to leave it at that, but I knew that I was going to have plenty of problems with General Daniel Makefa during the next few days, and I didn't believe in piling my plate too high. She finished her drink and stood up, and then made some awkward apologies until I cut her short. I saw her to the door and said,

"I trust that you were telling me the truth when you said that you had a room in this hotel? I don't want to know the number, but at this hour it might not be safe for you to go out unescorted."

She smiled a little. "It's all right, I do have a room here. Number three-twelve on the next floor."

I smiled too, and then I put my hands on her shoulders to hold her still, and kissed her gently on the mouth. It was a lovely mouth, the lips warm and sweet, but I knew that

I could not linger. I drew back and explained.

"You owed me that for keeping my promise to behave myself. Now you'd better go."

She nodded. "Good night, Mike."

"Good night, Virginia."

I let her out and she hurried away along the corridor. She didn't look back when she turned the corner and I closed the door and went back to the centre of the room. I stood there for a moment and wondered what it had all been about, and what her problem was. It was a puzzle, and I wasn't sure whether I wanted her to change her mind and come back to tell me all about it. Finally I realised that it was two o'clock in the morning and that my eyelids were drooping like lead weights, and so I went to bed.

By that I mean that I started to go to bed, but I got only as far as changing into my pyjamas before I heard the soft rapping of knuckles on the door. I straightened up and swore. It had been a frustrating night and I was irritable. I didn't want any more visitors.

I decided that if it was Virginia West returned then I would forget my fine moral principles and rape her. And if it was Lieutenant Kamau come to tuck me up and read me a bedtime story then I would tell him where to stuff his precious sense of duty and kick him down the lift shaft. With these nasty thoughts in mind I marched to the door and opened it.

I didn't find Virginia or Kamau. Instead I faced an unknown coloured gentleman, tall, politely smiling, and wearing a smart blue suit. I didn't immediately say or do anything nasty because there was a slight bulge under the left armpit of the smart blue suit which I wasn't naïve enough to diagnose as a peculiar attack of mumps. I'd been in the hardware business long enough to know when a man was wearing a shoulder holster, and it automatically followed so that inside the shoulder holster the man would be packing a gun.

Obviously the night wasn't yet over.

5

Polite Rebel

THE tall, dark stranger on my doorstep had impeccable manners and the most apologetic smile, despite his discreet taste in ironmongery. He said quietly,

"Good evening, Major M'Call. I'd like to come inside and speak with you if it isn't too inconvenient."

I asked sourly, "Isn't this a late hour to visit?"

"Very late, Major, and I apologise. But this is a strictly business call and very private. I think that you will understand."

He moved into my room as he spoke, not waiting for an invitation but smiling all the while to take any offence out of the action. He closed the door very gently behind him and then relaxed.

"You keep late hours, Major M'Call, otherwise I would have called earlier. I have been waiting for a long time in a rather uncomfortable broom cupboard just along the corridor. I saw you come in with the young lady, but of course it would have been indiscreet to disturb you until the lady had left."

"For that I suppose I should be grateful."

I was still in a vinegary mood but it was too late to throw him out. Besides which it would have been a direct contravention to two of my basic rules. One was never to be impolite to a man with a gun, even if he was keeping it hidden, and the other was never to refuse to discuss business. I offered him a chair which he accepted, but I didn't offer him a drink because I didn't want him to overstay his welcome. I sat down too and said bluntly,

"Now that you're here you'd better tell me who you are, and exactly what kind of business you want to discuss."

He smiled. "My name is Major

Sallah, and I am an army officer. And as for my business, I think we both know the kind of business in which you deal."

It was much too late in the morning for delicate fencing and I never have been shy about my trade. I continued to be blunt.

"I'm an arms dealer, Major Sallah. I represent the Trans-Global Arms Company and I sell guns and ammunition. Who do you represent, and what do you wish to buy?"

He smiled again. He was relaxed and polite and he wasn't going to be flustered or shaken. He said calmly,

"I understand that Trans-Global has contracted to provide the Federal Government with ten thousand rifles and fifty armoured cars. I think that if we could arrange a similar contract it would at least even up the balance."

"That means that *we* must be in opposition to the Federal Government."

Sallah nodded. "That is correct. I am an emissary for Major-General

Karagwe, the senior officer of the new Revolutionary Council of army officers in Kaduna. We expect the Federal Army to mobilise and make a determined attack on Kaduna as soon as they receive the arms shipment promised by Trans-Global, they especially need the armoured cars to give them more manoeuvrability. Therefore we need at least an equal arms build-up in order to defend ourselves."

"Defence is a word I never trust, especially as the best form of defence is attack. Your Revolutionary Council is illegal, and wouldn't it be more correct to state that you need more arms to defy the lawful Federal Government."

Sallah looked pained. "Major M'Call, I think that I should explain the Revolutionary Council's aim more fully, perhaps then you will have more sympathy with our position. In brief we have acted not with the intention of starting a civil war in Nigeria, but in the hope that we can avert one. Our country has been wracked with political and tribal jealousies ever since we first gained our independence in 1960. The Federation of Nigeria covers more than three hundred and fifty-six thousand square miles of West Africa, and comprises three different tribal regions. To the north the Hausas who are mainly Moslems, to the west the Yorubas, and to the east the Ibo peoples of Biafra. The present Federal Government is dominated by the north, which has the greater mass of population, but is less advanced in terms of education than the south. There is the initial cause for dissatisfaction, but the present Government is also corrupt and inefficient. Ministers who come to power owning a mud hut and a bicycle very quickly build themselves luxury villas and drive Rolls Royce cars. Last year general elections were held all over Nigeria which returned the present Government to power, but there was much rioting at the poll booths and many people believe that the elections were rigged. Nigeria is in fact one big, boiling pot that is all ready to explode. In Biafra there are rumours that the Ibos intend to break away from the Federation and form a separate government, and if that happens then there will be civil war. It is to prevent these things from happening, to change the Government while Nigeria is still in one piece, that the Revolutionary Council has acted."

He sounded very sincere, and perhaps he was. There were always a few who believed devoutly in the cause, just as there was always a majority who merely shouted the slogans while they grabbed a free ride to power. I didn't argue with him, but simply explained my position in turn.

"Major Sallah, those are noble sentiments, but you must realise that in the eyes of the world you and your people are still the rebels, challenging the legal Government of your country. All arms transactions are subject to clearance papers from their country of origin, and Trans-Global is a British company. I'm afraid that although you might convince me of your good faith, the British Government would never allow Trans-Global to supply you with arms. It simply isn't possible."

Sallah frowned, was silent for a moment, and then looked into my eyes. He said delicately,

"I know that what you say is true, but I also know that it is possible for normal regulations to be side-stepped or circumnavigated for discreet customers. I'm sure that with your experience you can at least advise me on how such things are done, and I can assure you that we shall be very discreet as to our source of supply."

I digested that, but for the moment I was feeling my way very tentatively round the whole situation, and I wasn't making any definite commitments. Instead I asked,

"Why come to me? In your case I would have thought that the Reds would be a more certain source of supply."

"You mean the Communists," Sallah smiled a little sadly. "I have no doubt that they would provide us with arms, but they would also wish to provide us with what they would term *advisers*, or offer training facilities in China or Russia where our young officers could be suitably indoctrinated at the same time. We are not Communists, Major M'Call, and we do not wish to be indebted to, or dependent upon the Communist world. Perhaps events will leave us no other choice, but if it is possible we would prefer to buy through you."

He stopped speaking, still looking me in the face, but I let him wait while I thought it over. I was tempted to fix myself another drink but decided against it. I had reached the stage where another one would dull rather than brighten my capacity for thought. Finally I said,

"It may be possible that I can help

you, but it is also too early to tell yet. I have to do a lot of thinking, and also I have to know more about the interests involved. There is one big question, and perhaps there you can help me?"

He hesitated, and then asked carefully, "What is the question?"

"It concerns Sir Stanley Okuwa, the Federal Premier. Your people kidnapped him during the revolt. I should very much like to know whether Okuwa is alive or dead? And if he is alive, then what does the Revolutionary Council intend to do with him?"

Sallah answered promptly because he had guessed at the coming question during that earlier hesitation. As he spoke he moved his shoulders in an apologetic shrug.

"I wish that I could help you, but even I do not know what has happened to the Premier. It is said that he was kidnapped by one of our groups, but communications are difficult in a country of this size, and our supporters are widely scattered. The central Revolutionary Council has no knowledge of Okuwa's present whereabouts."

"Then he was not taken to Kaduna?"

"No, he was not. His fate is a mystery to us also."

I didn't believe him, but my job had taught me sufficient diplomacy never to call anyone an outright liar. I put it another way.

"If he is alive, and he does fall into your hands, what would you do with him?"

"Negotiate," was the bland reply. "Our aims are limited. We have no wish to overthrow the Federal Government, but merely to clean it up. We wish to weed out some of the more corrupt ministers, to reshape Nigeria on a more democratic basis, and give our country a fresh start.

I thought of the two tribal chiefs, Kalewa and Seletso, and all the other guests who had attended Okuwa's ill-fated garden party, but I didn't ask whether murder was the only way to weed out corruption. Sallah and his friends obviously thought that it was. The Nigerian had paused, but when I didn't interrupt he went on.

"The truth will come to light in due course, that is inevitable. But in the meantime there is still the matter of our business, Major. It is unfortunate for the revolution that such a large section of the army has decided to continue to support the Federal Government, for now we really do have to fight to defend ourselves. We need arms. Will you supply them?"

I said slowly, "Purely as a matter of interest, how would I deliver?"

"It could be arranged." That polite, knowing smile was back on his smooth black face. "Delivery could be made to practically any part of West Africa, Ghana for instance, and then we could simply fly over the borders to collect."

"That's interesting." I returned his smile. "Perhaps I will give it some thought. If you care to contact me again within a couple of days then I might be prepared to discuss the whole thing a little further."

"But why is there any need for delay?"

I smiled again. "Let's say that I'm waiting for some real hard facts to emerge, especially about Sir Stanley Okuwa. I don't like to lay my bets on a race until I know how many horses are in the running."

Sallah's lips tightened a little. "Major M'Call, you must realise that I cannot make repeated visits to this hotel. I know that you are being watched. It is dangerous for me even to be in Lagos."

I said calmly, "Major Sallah, I do realise your position. But you must also realise mine. A deal of this kind cannot be promised on the spur of the moment, it needs thought and consideration. I must consult my company manager in London, and make certain enquiries. Even if I disregard the complication of the Premier's disappearance it will still take time."

Sallah was far from happy, but he had no room to argue. He frowned for a long moment, and then gave way with as much grace as possible.

"If that is the case, then it seems that I must take the risk of contacting you again."

"I'm sorry," I said. "But I can't say any more at this stage. Give me a couple of days, and then I should be able to give you a definite yes or no answer."

Sallah nodded dubiously, and then after a moment he got to his feet. He was reluctant to go but he knew that he could make no further advances tonight. We shook hands and said a few more polite but irrelevant things, and then I saw him to the door. I warned him about Kamau, but he seemed quite confident of remaining unobserved as he took his leave.

When he had gone I went into the bathroom to clean my teeth, and then I made my long-delayed climb into bed. During the teeth-cleaning operation I tried to fit Major Sallah into one of my mental file cards but it was difficult. There was no general background and he talked too smoothly for me to be very sure of anything he had said. I gave it up when I got into bed, switched out the light, and wearily closed my eyes.

I couldn't sleep. I was tired and drained, but even in the quiet darkness my mind refused to rest. I had stopped trying to analyse Sallah, but I was still wondering over his visit, and wondering most of all whether I could in fact pull off a neat double by selling to both sides of the Nigerian conflict at the same time. As an official representative of Trans-Global I knew that the rebels were out of bounds, the company wouldn't touch them. But a little private enterprise through private contacts and something might be done.

Behind my closed eyes my brain was aching, but stubbornly it persisted in turning the same greedy circles.

6

Black News

THE next morning there was a great buzz of excitement running through the streets of Lagos, but I overslept and missed the radio broadcast that had caused it. However, I wasn't allowed to oversleep for long. The broadcast came at 9 a.m., and at nine-thirty Lieutenant Kamau was hammering at my door. He made such a racket that I thought that the rebels had at least invaded the city. It was impossible to ignore him so I crawled out of bed to let him in.

He said brightly, "Good morning, Major M'Call."

I glowered at him. I'm never at my best in the morning, especially with smart black lieutenants who salute as though they've just stepped off the parade ground at Sandhurst. They give me a complex. I said threateningly,

"Good morning, Lieutenant Kamau."

His mission was too urgent to worry about the temperament of a grumpy arms dealer. He probably didn't even notice. He asked quickly,

"Have you heard the radio this morning, sir? Did you hear the rebel announcement from Kaduna?"

I took interest, and shook my head.

"The message came from the traitor, Major-General Karagwe, speaking on behalf of what he called the Revolutionary Council. It was mostly blatant propaganda and distortion of the true facts, but at last they admit that Premier Okuwa is dead." He made a darkly significant pause, and then finished, "General Makefa wishes to see you immediately. I have the car waiting outside."

I was silent for a moment, thinking about Sir Stanley Okuwa and the useless stupidity of it all. For the moment I didn't even want to hear the details of his death, it was enough that one of Africa's greatest statesmen, and Nigeria's only hope, was dead. Then my cynicism came back and I asked myself what else had I expected. At least now the situation would become clearer, and my job might be easier. I looked at Kamau and said,

"You'd better come inside and wait while I get showered and dressed." I turned away, and then added as an afterthought, "While you're waiting you can ring down room service, and tell them to send up a big pot of coffee."

★ ★ ★

Half an hour later we went down to the car and drove out to Army H.Q. The sun was hot, grilling the city and reflecting blinding flashes from the lagoon. In the streets the normal routine had slowed noticeably and again there were heavy troop congestions on every corner. Today the black faces of the soldiers looked more grim, and they looked to be more itchy-fingered on the trigger. Kamau drove fast and in silence, and now that I was awake I noticed that there was a holstered revolver at his hip.

I was quite prepared to find Makefa in the same grim mood, and I was not to be disappointed. The General was again entrenched behind that massive oak desk when we arrived, but he made the gesture of rising to greet us. I was invited to sit, while Kamau was thanked and dismissed. When the lieutenant had gone Makefa squared his shoulders and rested his hands upon the desk, the perfect picture of the strong man unbowed by the heavy burdens of destiny. He said sombrely,

"Our Premier has been murdered. This is a black day for Nigeria, perhaps for the whole of Africa."

I nodded, I couldn't argue with that.

"Did you hear the actual broadcast, Major M'Call?"

I shook my head. "No, I was still in

103

bed. Lieutenant Kamau just told me the bare facts."

"Then perhaps I should tell you exactly what has happened, or at least as much as can be believed. The traitor officers in Kaduna have formed what they call a Revolutionary Council, headed by a Major-General Karagwe. They made their second radio announcement this morning. First they repeated their previous untrue accusations about corruption and bribery, etcetera, which they claim is rife in the present Government. Secondly they called upon myself and all loyal officers and men of the Federal Army to turn traitor and join them in their cause, which they describe as re-shaping a new and free Nigeria. Third they reported the death of Sir Stanley Okuwa."

Here Makefa paused, his thick lips tightening and his face filling with thunder. He leaned forward and continued,

"I must tell you, Major M'Call that they have shamefully misrepresented the facts of the Premier's death. I received reports late last night which prove that Sir Stanley was taken north of Kaduna. He was ill-treated and beaten-up because they thought that they could force him to cooperate with their aims. He made a desperate effort to escape and was shot dead by some of the common soldiers before their officers could intervene. Those are the true facts, but they have been twisted to the reverse. The rebels dare to suggest that the troops who kidnapped the Premier and murdered his guests and his servants were not part of their supporters at all. They suggest that those troops were under my command and that I had the Premier taken away into the jungle and executed him."

I said in my most prudent voice, "Why would you want to do that?"

"They claim that I wanted Okuwa dead so that I could take command, and also so that I can blame the rebels for his death. This is all so obviously untrue that I do not even have to deny it."

It wasn't so obvious to me, but I nodded in soothing agreement. I didn't even ask him for the source of his own reports on which he based his version of Okuwa's death, for that would have been tactless. Okuwa was almost certainly dead, and I was beginning to think that the truth of it didn't even matter. The only real truth was that both sides were hell-bent on a war for the crown, and I wasn't prepared to believe in anything other than that.

Makefa hesitated for a moment, as though he had hoped for some definite comment, and then he decided to go on.

"This new development is a serious one, Major. It has deeper aspects than is at first evident. Perhaps you are aware that Sir Stanley Okuwa was a Hausa and a Moslem. There are twenty-nine million Moslems in Nigeria who regarded him as their champion and their leader, and if they should decide to avenge his death then the bloodshed could be terrible. Fortunately we are now entering the period of Ramadan, the Moslem fast during which they are forbidden to eat, drink, smoke, or indulge in any form of sexual activity between dawn and sunset. They are also forbidden to perform any acts of violence. So we are safe until the end of the month of Ramadan, but when those religious restrictions are lifted anything can happen. Some Moslems may believe the rebel lies and exact their vengeance upon the Government supporters and the loyal army. Others may believe the truth and rise against the rebel forces. And others may simply cry for a holy war and slaughter any non-Moslems they can find, regardless of their politics. Do you begin to understand the extent of my fears?"

I nodded, I was understanding only too well. The whole mess was getting even more complicated, and the end of Ramadan would be a damned good time to be out of the country, preferably right out of Africa.

Makefa regarded me gravely and said, "If you understand then you realise why I must have those arms promised to me by Trans-Global without any further delay. The fast of Ramadan now gives me a time limit in which to crush this rebellion and bring the murderers of Sir Stanley Okuwa to justice. As you say in your English courts, justice must be done and be seen to be done. It is the only way to avert a Moslem uprising."

"You have a good argument," I admitted. "And now that I have some definite facts to report to my company they should be able to persuade the British Government to release those arms. I'll arrange a call to London as soon as I get back to my hotel."

Makefa smiled for the first time. "That won't be necessary, Major. I have already taken the liberty of arranging that call for you." He glanced at his wristwatch and added, "It should come through in thirty minutes, and to save you the wasted journey to your hotel it can be taken here." As he spoke he reached out and patted one of the two black telephones on his desk.

★ ★ ★

The call was late and three-quarters of an hour passed before the telephone actually rang. Makefa answered it, listened for a moment, thanked the operator and then passed the receiver to me.

"Your call is through, Major." He paused and then asked, "Would it be easier to consult your employers in private? If you wish I can leave you alone."

I made a negative smile. He was so compliant that the call was probably being recorded anyway. I told him that it wasn't necessary in my best nothing-to-hide style and he smiled too. He sat back in his chair and waited.

It was Murchison on the other end of the line. That Scottish growl was recognisable anywhere, even above the squeaks and pips and peculiar humming noises of the Nigerian telephone service. I could even guess that his digestive system was troubling him again. We exchanged brief courtesies and then he listened while I said my piece. I explained that I was speaking from Makefa's office to forestall any tactless questions, and then gave him a condensed account of the morning's developments, strictly from the official viewpoint. Murchison cursed the faulty line a couple of times, demanding that I repeat myself or speak up, but he had only one definite question.

"Mike, are you sure that Okuwa is out of the picture?"

"It seems pretty definite. Makefa's reports and the rebel announcement both state that he's dead."

There was a distant grunt, and then silence for thought. Vague noises still filtered through to my ear, but I wasn't sure whether they were atmospherics or Murchison's stomach. Finally he said,

"If that's true then General Makefa must be the sole lawful authority in Nigeria, he already has the approval of the Federal cabinet to run the country. I can put that to the Foreign Office and should be able to get those arms released in a matter of hours. Clearance should only be a formality now. You can pass that information to the General."

I turned and told Makefa. His face showed angry impatience and he snapped tartly "Surely there can be no further delays. It is vital that I take full control of my country as soon as possible, and I need those armoured cars and rifles. I cannot afford to lose time over these stupid formalities."

I nodded and raised the receiver again.

"Tom, the situation is pretty dodgy out here. There's a serious threat of Moslem violence to avenge the death of Okuwa, and Makefa needs those arms fast. Can't you anticipate the F.O. decision and release those arms now?"

I could imagine Murchison shaking his head, just as I had known he would.

"You know I can't do that, Mike. I could get Trans-Global black-listed out of business if I made a habit of anticipating decisions. The best I can do is to get on to the Foreign Office and try to hurry them up a bit. They should have the latest news through from their own sources, so they won't have a lot of room to argue. I'll put another call through to Lagos this afternoon and let you know what develops."

"In that case you'd best put it through to the Ambassadors Hotel, I'll probably be there." I was aware of Makefa fuming on the opposite side of the desk and added a parting shot.

"Push this one hard, Tom. This shipment is really important. Nigeria needs it badly and we can't afford to lose a customer."

Murchison said something that sounded like, "Do my best," but it

112

was mostly blotted out by a sudden whine. We both said good-bye and then hung up.

Then I had to suffer more protests from the frustrated Makefa. I was beginning to feel sorry for him but there was nothing that I could do.

★ ★ ★

I escaped after another ten minutes, and outside Kamau was again waiting for me like the faithful watchdog he had become. We both climbed into the Jaguar and he drove me back to the island city and the Ambassadors Hotel. There I went through the pointless routine of telling him that I wouldn't be needing him again until much later in the afternoon, and he saluted smartly and pretended that we weren't both aware that he would be hovering close to the hotel anyway.

I went inside, sauntered up to my room, and spent a token thirty minutes in lying on my bed and doing some strenuous thinking. My thoughts covered a lot of territory but at last I arrived at one tentative decision. I got on to my feet again and cautiously descended to the foyer.

I avoided the lift and used the stairs instead. The two clerks behind the reception desk were both busy, the doorman was facing outwards to the forecourt, and nobody seemed to be paying any attention to me. I turned left and made my way out through a side exit, trying hard to look as though I wasn't being furtive. There was no sign of Kamau but he couldn't be everywhere at once and I was gambling that I wasn't worth more than one man to look after me. I hurried away and convinced myself that all the sweat that was seeping out of me was due solely to the malarial heat.

It took me twenty minutes to walk to the External Telecommunications centre and there I went inside and made out three brief cables. They went to different parts of Europe, two to

France and one to Italy, but all three were addressed to contacts I had made in the more shady areas of my trade. They were all private dealers in arms and ammunition. The message was contained in just two cryptic words: *Any spares?* Translated they meant simply, do you have any stocks that are not subject to normal clearance papers.

I had decided that if General Makefa was in an urgent panic, then Major Sallah would be in an urgent panic too. And as I hadn't yet decided who was in the right the least that I could do was to maintain the balance between them.

7

Girl Gone

I GOT back to the hotel without attracting any attention and went thankfully into the lounge bar for a couple of ice-cold beers. Around me there was a lot of talk about the rebel radio speech from Kaduna but I wasn't tempted to take part. I had no interest in a confused mess of biased opinions and I doubted if anyone knew any real facts. I took my beer into a cool corner and gave myself a rest.

When I had first started dealing in arms I did have a few scraps of moral conscience. I thought that I should only sell guns to the good guys and not to the bad guys. Then I got played for a sucker a couple of times in the Middle East. The sincere and idealistic reformers who had convinced me that they had only the collective good of their peoples at heart had proved to be the blackest villains imaginable just as soon as they had armed their supporters with a shipload of automatic weapons. It just wasn't possible to divide the good guys from the bad guys. The attacking wolves and the defending sheep all looked and sounded exactly the same. For a man who was such a lousy judge of human nature as I was, moral conscience was a waste of time. I decided then that the only way to hold any genuine, unhypocritical moral conscience was to stay out of arms dealing altogether, otherwise I might just as well sell to anybody who wanted to buy. I thought about that for a while but it left me with no real choice. I had spent most of my adult life handling weapons of one sort or another, and I didn't know anything else. I could never have sold insurance policies to suspicious housewives as efficiently as I sold guns or tanks to scheming generals. Having settled that in my own mind I now regarded dealing in arms as just another business, and as much as possible I tried to stay uninvolved with the wider issues. If anyone asked me I compared arming both sides to a shoe salesman selling football boots to both Manchester City and Manchester United. The game would be played and the result would not depend one iota upon whose boots they were wearing, just as the battle would be fought and it didn't matter who supplied the guns. If I didn't provide them then someone else would.

I revised this crude philosophy and found myself basically still satisfied. The very fact that I needed to revise it meant that I was having pangs of conscience over the prospects of dealing with Sallah, but there was no denying the one mountainous truth. People who made weapons to kill, or sold weapons to kill, could have no morals. If they tried they were hypocrites. At least I was honest enough with myself not to be a hypocrite.

I put a brake on my thinking there, before I could stumble over another thought that might upset the whole balance of my logic. I had another beer and then I wandered into the hotel restaurant to eat. Afterwards there was nothing that I wanted to see or do in Lagos, and also I couldn't face the afternoon heat. I went up to my room, switched on the ceiling fan at full speed and indulged in the old Spanish habit of siesta. I was doing most of my living at night so it seemed the sensible thing to do.

I was interrupted after thirty minutes. I recognised the brisk, vigorous knock and groaned because I knew I couldn't ignore it. He wouldn't go away. I got up with an effort and went to open the door.

Lieutenant Kamau smiled at me, the smile I was beginning to detest. He wasn't alone and I paid most of my attention to his friend. The second man matched Kamau for size and weight, but he was an older man with a more serious face, and his Negro features more clearly marked. He too wore a uniform but it wasn't the uniform of the Federal Army. His trousers were black, his shirt grey with shiny silver epaulettes, and he wore a black peaked cap. Like Kamau he carried a revolver holstered at his right hip. A dark bird of foreboding twittered in my ear and told me that he spelled trouble.

Kamau said cheerfully, "Major M'Call, may I introduce Captain Shabani of the Lagos Police. If it is convenient he would like to ask you a few questions."

It wasn't convenient, and I didn't want to answer any questions. I know that policemen are wonderful and necessary, but I have always preferred them to do their duty without any help from me. It's a guilt complex that stems from the day that a ten-foot sergeant accompanied an equally tall and violently red-faced farmer up my mother's garden path in search of the very little boy who had been stealing pears. However, M'Call the man was now in command, and in any case I would have looked silly trying to hide under the bed. I said flippantly,

"Why, what exactly have I done?"

"Nothing I hope." Shabani didn't need Kamau to speak for him, and his smile was just a polite concession, it didn't last for more than two seconds. Then he added, "But I think you may be able to help me with some enquiries."

We looked at each other, sized up what we saw, and I don't think either of us fell in love. I shrugged my shoulders and moved aside to let them in. Shabani removed his cap and stood comfortably at ease and Kamau decided to follow his example. I closed the door and waited for one of them to speak. Shabani began smoothly.

"Major M'Call, I am trying to find a certain young lady, a white girl, English I think, but I do not know any more about her. I only know that you were in the company of this young lady last night, or at least in the company of a young lady who fits this description. Can you tell me her name, please?"

I was suddenly alert. I hadn't thought any more about Virginia West since we had said good-bye last night, but now it was beginning to look as though I had not wholly escaped from her undisclosed problem. I looked darkly at Kamau, wondering at his part in this unexpected call. Had he approached Shabani, or had the policeman approached him? The lieutenant returned my gaze innocently and I knew that it was irrelevant. The basic fact was that Shabani was here and I had to make some answer to the question. I could hardly pretend that I did not know the girl by name, and to have made up a false name would have meant speaking a lie that could be proved against me later. Direct lies mean complications that can boomerang with sticky results and I avoid them whenever possible. I said frankly,

"Her name was Virginia West."

Shabani frowned, the name obviously meant nothing.

"Do you know where I can find this lady now? Do you know where she is staying?"

Obviously he also didn't know that she had a room here at the Ambassadors, or was he trying to catch me out. I decided that that was unlikely and so I choose not to enlighten him. I had liked the girl, despite the frustrations of her visit, and there was no need to be a complete cad. I shook my head unhelpfully and said in my best honest-john voice,

"I'm sorry, Captain, but there I can't help you. That's one of the things she didn't tell me."

"But you have arranged to meet again?"

I repeated the head-shake. "Unfortunately no. I met Miss West for the first time last night, in the bar of this hotel. We drove out to the beach as Lieutenant Kamau has probably told you. We went swimming, but afterwards we had a slight disagreement." I paused to leer faintly. Let him think I was a lecher. I didn't care. "After that we came back here. It was her car. I persuaded her to have a final drink, but after that she left. She didn't want to see me again."

"Then your relationship with this girl was just a casual one." Shabani made his doubt plain. "You had not met her previously?"

I could answer that with a clear conscience.

"That's the way it was."

"Yet she went to the 'Blue Oasis' while you were there, and also she was waiting in the bar of this hotel when you returned. Is that not a strange coincidence?"

"Perhaps, and perhaps she wasn't deliberately waiting for me. Perhaps she just haunts bars."

"Perhaps." Shabani put a different stress on the word and didn't sound convinced. "What did she tell you about herself?"

"Nothing." I did my leer again. "I wasn't interested in her past history. I had other things on my mind."

"But she must have told you something."

I grinned. "She did. But mostly she told me what I was."

I was enjoying this but Shabani wasn't. He was getting nowhere fast. He said grimly,

"And you say that you will not be meeting her again."

"That's right. I'm a busy man, Captain. I'm here to talk business with General Makefa." I knew that that was precisely why I could be uncooperative and get away with it, so I chucked it in as though he didn't know. "Lieutenant Kamau will verify that for you. My stay in Lagos will be short and my talks with the General don't leave me much time, that's why I didn't press this girl to let me see her again."

"I see," Shabani glowered. "You say that this girl drove her own car. What make was the car, please?"

I said promptly, "It was a Ford Cortina, fairly new." A Cortina was far enough from a Corsair to confuse any search, and close enough for me to plead a genuine mistake if it became necessary.

Shabani had run out of questions, or else he saw no further point as he was not getting any satisfactory answers. He put on his cap and said coldly,

"Thank you, Major M'Call. It does not seem that you can be of any definite help to my enquiries, but I am grateful for your assistance." He stressed that last word, but I smiled as though I really had been trying to help. He finished without any real hope, "If you should chance to meet with this young lady — this Virginia West — once again, please let me know. You can contact me at Lagos Police

Headquarters, or through Lieutenant Kamau."

"Certainly, Captain." I saw them to the door and then asked as an afterthought, "Just as a matter of interest, what has the girl done? Why do you want to find her?"

"Perhaps she has done nothing, Major. Until we find her we cannot even be sure that she is the person for whom we are looking."

His thick lips curled into a faint smile and I knew that he found some compensation in being able to play the wise guy in turn. He wasn't going to enlighten me any more than I had been prepared to enlighten him. The snag was that I couldn't press him without spoiling all that casual act I had just made, and he knew that too. I tried once more by just rephrasing the question.

"This girl for whom you are looking — what has *she* done?"

"Again it is difficult to say until we find her. I merely believe that she can help with my enquiries."

He waited for me to speak again but two questions was my limit. If I made it three then he would have grounds for believing that I did have an interest in Virginia West, and that perhaps I did expect to see her again. Then I would find myself back on the receiving end. I shrugged and said,

"Then I wish you luck. If I should see the girl anywhere I'll let you know. Good-bye, Captain Shabani."

Shabani touched his cap in a brief salute.

"Good-bye, Major M'Call."

I let them out but Kamau hung back for a moment, looking vaguely uncomfortable as though he had been an unwilling witness. It was never easy sitting astride a fence. I smiled to prove we were still friends and said,

"You'd best call back in a couple of hours. I should get a call through from London by then, and I may have some news for the General. I'll want the car."

Kamau looked happier, saluted smartly, and then walked away after Shabani.

I closed the door behind them, waited two minutes, and then looked out into the corridor again. They had gone but I checked around in both directions to make sure that they weren't hiding somewhere, and watching for me to do something stupid. When I was satisfied that they must have descended to the foyer I did the something stupid and ran up fast to the fourth floor. Virginia had said that her room was at the back of the hotel, and with that clue in mind it took me less than half a minute to find number three-twelve.

I rapped gently with my knuckles on the door. There was no answer and after a moment I knocked more loudly. Still no answer and I began throwing anxious glances back along the passageway. It was more than possible that Shabani would check at the hotel desk on his way out, and now that he had her name they would send him right up here. I had the pear-stealing jitters again and I didn't want to be caught in the act. I knocked a third time and hopefully tried the door.

It opened and I stood there uncertainly for another second. Virginia might not have been telling me the truth when she had said that she was staying here, and I didn't want to barge in on some strange female sleeping through the afternoon heat. Strange females had nasty habits of screaming when awoken by intruders and even strange men could get justifiably annoyed. Then I told myself that dithering could be fatal and went in.

It was just a single room with a bed, dressing-table and wardrobe, and an adjoining shower. Fortunately, or unfortunately, in that moment I wasn't sure which, the bed was empty. I let another second waste and then I started on some hurried detective work. In the shower I found the white bathing suit she had worn last night, and in the wardrobe I recognised her golden dress, so at least Virginia had not been lying when she told me that this was her room.

There were two other dresses in the wardrobe, both simple cotton frocks that looked as though they had been washed many times. The golden sheath was the only thing suitable for night life and that had not been worn too often. I checked the dressing-table but the drawers were empty, while the glass tray in front of the mirror bore only a few jars and tubes of cosmetics and a neatly arranged set of hair brushes. There was a leather suitcase under the bed, heavy and locked. I fiddled with it for a moment, then realised that I couldn't spare the time and pushed it back where it belonged. I had learned nothing except that Virginia West was no spoiled little rich girl, and that the sophisticated air she had put on earlier last night had been purely an act.

With that I had to be satisfied and I got out as quickly as I came in. I couldn't warn her if she wasn't there, and keeping a wary eye open for Shabani I returned to the third floor. Here I stalled and gave myself more time to think.

The facts were uncomfortable. Virginia was in trouble. The police were after her and she was missing from her room, and the fact that she had not locked her door seemed to indicate that she had left in a hurry. It wasn't really any of my business but I couldn't just go back to my room and skulk out of the way. The businessman part of me said that I should, but damsels in distress have a harrowing effect on what's left of my shrunken conscience, especially the pretty ones. I finally called myself a fool and went down to the foyer.

There was no sign of either Shabani or Kamau so I went direct to the reception desk. I bore in mind that they might have been here before me and phrased my questions carefully to the inquiring clerk.

"I'm looking for a young English girl named Virginia West. I met her in the lounge bar last night. Can you tell me if she is staying at the hotel?"

The clerk was helpful, he consulted his book and told me what I already knew. Also he showed no special interest or curiosity in my query, which he no doubt would have done if he had been asked the same question by the police during the past five minutes. I felt more hopeful that Shabani had left the hotel, but I had to remember that he could always come back. I asked innocently,

"Can you tell me if she is in the hotel now?"

"I'll call her room for you, sir, and check."

He smiled politely and picked up his telephone, and I had to wait while he made the unanswered call. However, I had the answer that I wanted. He hadn't seen her go out and so he wouldn't know where I could find her. When he put the phone down and made his negative report I thanked him and commented that I would try again later. Then I started to turn away, wondering what, if anything, I could do next. The clerk raised his voice slightly to bring me back.

"Major M'Call, there is a message for you."

I stopped and he rummaged in the rack of initialled boxes behind him to produce a sealed white envelope that bore my name and the address of the Ambassadors Hotel. He passed it over the desk and I asked,

"Who delivered it?"

"An African boy, sir, from outside the hotel."

I thanked him again, and then moved away to slit open the envelope. Inside there was a folded note with two lines in block capitals:

PLEASE COME TO THE ZAMBESI COFFEE BAR THIS AFTERNOON. IT IS VERY IMPORTANT.

There was nothing else, not even a signature.

8

Deal Closed

I KNEW the 'Zambesi'. I remembered that it was down on the seafront looking out to the lagoon. The clerk was watching me so I didn't go there right away. Instead I went back to my room and killed a few more minutes before making another furtive descent by the stairs. When I re-entered the foyer I almost collided with Kamau. He had probably seen Shabani off the premises and was coming back through the main glass doors. I recognised his peaked cap and army uniform and did a smart side-step behind a nearby column. Kamau circled the mermaid fountain, but fortunately he wasn't looking for me. He turned into the lounge and I guessed that that was where he sat and waited during most of his spare time. He probably watched the foyer which I would have to cross to go out through the main doors, and he wasn't yet aware that I had any real reasons for doing sneaky things like using the side exits. I waited a minute to make sure that he had settled down and then used the side door again.

It took me thirty minutes to reach the 'Zambesi' and when I got there I was hot and sweating. I had hurried because I had to be back before my call came through from Murchison in London, and hurrying on a sweltering West African afternoon isn't exactly good for the temper. The coffee bar was one of those new sophisticated places that served creamy teacakes and crystallised fruits in a cool expensive atmosphere. It was a relief to get inside where there was air conditioning, and I looked around expecting to see Virginia.

She wasn't there. Instead I recognised Major Sallah.

He sat alone in a corner, isolated

from the few other customers, and sudden dark thoughts flirted through my mind. I decided there and then that if Sallah was responsible for the disappearance of Virginia West then I would bust him in two and throw the pieces to Makefa. Not immediately of course, but as soon as I was sure that she was safe. I went over to his table and sat down.

Sallah was wearing his dark blue suit and a thin tie, and looked much cooler than I felt in my shirt sleeves. He smiled at me and said,

"You received my message, Major. Thank you for coming."

I wasn't flattered or soothed by that smile. I said bluntly,

"What's it about?"

"The same matter as before. You must have heard the radio announcement from Kaduna this morning, and I know that you were called to see General Makefa immediately afterwards. I don't doubt that Makefa denied the Revolutionary Council's announcement, but I can assure you that our version of the facts is the correct one. However, last night you needed to know whether Sir Stanley Okuwa was alive or dead. Today you know that he is dead, murdered by troops under Makefa's command. You have also had the time that you need to think over my business proposition. Now I need to know your answer."

There was an interruption as a young Negress asked for my order. It was too hot for coffee, and I settled for an iced lime squash. When she had gone away again I said,

"Major Sallah, I have the feeling that you are being devious with me. Last night you claimed absolutely no knowledge of the Premier's fate. Today the whole of Nigeria, in fact the whole world, is told that he is dead."

Sallah nodded. "That is true, but you must appreciate that private communications are difficult between here and Kaduna. I am somewhat isolated from my brother officers on the Revolutionary Council."

"So you only know what you heard on the radio this morning, and you believe it?"

If he had not worn that polite mask he would have shown anger, and he answered firmly, "That broadcast was made by Major-General Karagwe. He is not only our leader but my personal friend. I trust him implicitly."

There was another delay while the girl brought my iced drink, and then Sallah went on,

"I assure you, Major M'Call, that I have been perfectly frank with you. You know as much as I know myself. The only difference is that I have a closer knowledge of both Karagwe and Makefa, and I know which of them to believe. What must be obvious to both of us now is that events in Nigeria are coming to a head. There was a pause in time while the fate of Sir Stanley Okuwa was unknown, but now history is beginning to move forward once again. That is why I must press you for a decision. You know my task, will you or will you not help me to accomplish it?"

I said slowly, "I explained last night that these things take time. I have to make enquiries and find out what stocks are available. I haven't made a decision yet."

The polite mask began to slip, and some of the anger and frustration began to show through. To a small extent that made me feel somewhat better, for it assured me that he didn't have Virginia West. If he had abducted her to use as some kind of lever against me he would have mentioned her name by now. Sallah obviously had no levers at all.

"You'll just have to wait," I told him. "My kind of business doesn't result in overnight sales. And the next time you send me a message I suggest that you put your name at the bottom. I'm always happier when I know who to expect."

"That would not have been wise." He spoke as though he was trying hard to sound patient. "If the wrong people had read it they would have wondered why I wanted to contact you. Also it is not safe for me to visit your hotel. Lieutenant Kamau is a capable, although misguided young officer, and I remember him with respect. An unsigned letter was my only choice. The next time you will know who to expect."

I said flatly, "There isn't going to be any next time. I don't feel any easier about dodging Kamau to get out than you feel about dodging him to get in. Also there's no point in holding any more of these conversations until I do make a decision. I'll try and meet you here at the same time in two days, perhaps by then we'll have something to discuss. Until then it's best for both of us if you don't try to contact me at all."

"Two days!" Sallah looked agitated. "So much can happen in two days, and the Revolutionary Council are already pressing me for a definite reply."

"I'm sorry, Major Sallah, but that's as much as I can say."

I couldn't do the impossible and he should have known it. Also I was tired of arguing with him, and annoyed that he had dragged me out here for nothing. To add the final layer of my irritability I still had Virginia West on my mind. I drank the last of my lime squash, stood up, and told him firmly,

"Right now I have to get back to my hotel. I'm expecting a call from my head office in London, and if I'm not there to take it then the management will start looking for me. That means that Lieutenant Kamau will be looking too, and we don't want that."

Sallah nodded, he wasn't at all happy, but in the circumstances there was nothing he could do. It was a seller's market. He said with great reluctance,

"Then two days it must be."

I agreed. "Two days will be fine, here at the 'Zambesi'."

We parted less cordially and this time

142

we didn't shake hands. Sallah stayed behind and I could feel him watching me all the way to the door. Outside it was still hot.

★ ★ ★

I hurried back to the Ambassadors, and once I had regained my room I indulged in the luxury of a cold shower. It didn't matter now if I took the London call wet and naked, just as long as I was here to take it. Afterwards I put on a clean shirt, pants, socks and trousers, and felt refreshingly human, even though I knew that the feeling wouldn't last five minutes. I stared at the telephone for a moment, and its silence convinced me that I could risk another two-minute absence. I went up to the fourth floor and checked number three-twelve for the second time, but again it was unlocked and empty. There was no sign that Virginia had ever returned so I didn't linger.

Back in my room I mixed the first

real drink of the day, and wondered what I could possibly do on her behalf. Having refused to help Shabani find her I could hardly go to the police now and report her missing. The girl was looming larger in my thoughts than all my other problems put together, but a long stretch of concentrated thinking failed to bring me any nearer to any definite decision.

Finally the telephone rang, and I had my connection with Murchison, three thousand miles away on the other end of the line. We talked for fifteen minutes.

* * *

When we had finished I went downstairs to find Kamau but it was an unnecessary move. The lieutenant was already on his way up to meet me. The reception desk must have informed him that my call had come through, and Makefa had obviously given instructions that as soon as that happened I should be

brought back to Army H.Q. Kamau
smiled hopefully and asked,

"You have some news for the
General?"

"I have some very good news for the
General." I felt like smiling too because
now I could get at least one man off my
back. I added cheerfully, "Let's go and
tell him all about it."

Kamau did an about turn and fell
into step beside me. We went outside
to the waiting staff car and made
the now familiar journey out of the
city. I wasn't even impressed by the
lurking troops and guns any more, so
much does familiarity breed contempt.
They were all a mere part of the
accepted scene. We were now just
as well known at the gates and were
waved into the army camp after a
casually formal halt. The word had
gone ahead, probably telephoned by
Kamau, or perhaps the exchange had
orders to report direct whenever I
received any calls. Whatever the answer
I was expected and ushered straight

into Makefa's office. He was smiling as though he already knew the results of my conversation with Murchison, which meant that he probably did. I was offered a chair as though it was a throne and I was a visiting prince.

I said my piece. "General, I'm pleased to report that the delays are over. Mister Murchison, Trans-Global's managing director at head office saw his Foreign Office contact immediately after my earlier call this morning. He had to wait for further talks and consultations, but finally we have permission to release those arms. The clearance papers were already in order so all we needed was the verbal signal to go ahead. Murchison has already contacted the shipowners of the *African Rose*, and they are cabling instructions to the ship's captain. She's due to sail from Freetown at midnight, and Lagos will be her next port of call."

Makefa was all smiles. He said with

satisfaction, "Then I can expect delivery in three days?"

I nodded. "Add a day for unloading, and you can strengthen your troops and send them north on the fifth."

"That is excellent, Major M'Call." Makefa reached underneath his desk and produced a brand-new bottle of whisky and two glasses. He broke the golden seal, beamed and said, "This calls for a celebration. Will you drink scotch?"

I would and I said so. Makefa poured two glasses, did his conjuring trick again and brought out a soda syphon to weaken them a bit, and then we toasted the swift return to order of the troubled Federation of Nigeria. Makefa drank and then asked,

"Now that our deal is satisfactorily closed, when will you be leaving Lagos?"

I smiled. "Not for another three days. It's part of my job to check the shipment on arrival, and if you remember it was a payment on delivery agreement. I also have to pick up the cheque."

Makefa laughed. "I was hoping that you would forget that, but if you are staying then I will leave Lieutenant Kamau and the staff car at your disposal. It would be rude of me to withdraw him simply because we no longer need to keep so closely in touch."

I thanked him for his consideration and we both smiled again and drank more whisky. At the same time I wondered whether he suspected that I had been approached, or that I might be approached by the rebels. If that was so then perhaps he was keeping a close check on all my incoming calls and cables as well as upon my person. I sincerely hoped not, because the answers to those *any spares* signals, no matter how discreetly worded, might take a lot of explaining.

9

Deadline Ramadan

AFTER three large helpings of scotch, a vigorous handshake and several hearty slaps on the back I finally escaped from Makefa's office. I left behind a very happy General, and Kamau too was all smiles as he drove me back to the hotel. He didn't need to be listening at the door, for anyone could have read the signs on our faces as Makefa and I emerged. Kamau was hopeful that he would be given command of one of the new armoured cars when the Army moved north to recapture Kano and Kaduna, and he chattered all the way back into Lagos. He had youth and the conviction of right on his side, and he was confident of victory. I listened to him and hoped that he would live long enough to grow wise; wise enough to know that there was often right on both sides, and that consequently the righteous sometimes had to lose. Perhaps then he would learn understanding, instead of patriotic hatred for his enemies. If enough firebrands like Kamau lived to grow wise, then there might be hope for Africa yet.

I reflected that the lieutenant and Major Sallah were in many respects two of a kind. They had the same sincerity, and the same dedicated belief that they were following the right course. If they met tomorrow they would probably fight to the death, but if they survived through time to understanding it was equally possible that they would emerge as allies. Peace was always a compromise. It was a pity that the odds were all against their surviving, and that even if they did survive there would be other adolescent firebrands taking up their discarded cries for blood and revolution. My cynicism was coming back because it was easier to bear. Life held no disillusion or disappointment for a cynic.

My thoughts and Kamau's chatter lasted us all the way back to the hotel. There I again dismissed him for the rest of the evening and he made a diplomatic pretence of accepting my dismissal. Then I went up to my room.

It was then about five o'clock, too early to think about dinner and yet there wasn't much that I could do with the tail-end of the afternoon. The temperature was still hovering around in the upper eighties and so I decided to relax and finish my interrupted siesta. I walked into the bedroom and thankfully stripped off my shirt, and as I did so I heard a faint sound in the bathroom.

I listened but it didn't come again. In any other African hotel I might have put it down to a lizard or a cockroach scuttling up the wall, but not here in the Ambassadors. Besides, lizards and cockroaches made repeated scuttling sounds, and whatever was in my bathroom had frozen into silence.

I stood for a moment and then walked over to the dressing-table beside my bed. I pulled out the second drawer down, turned over a small pile of spare clothes, and lifted out the Browning P-35 in its holster. I left the holster on the bed, but I took the Browning with me to investigate the bathroom. The gun was already loaded and I pulled back the slide to lift a round into position before I put my head round the door.

At first sight the bathroom appeared to be empty, but the shower curtain was drawn and I knew I hadn't left it that way. I also worked it out that the sound I had heard could quite logically have been the shower curtain moving. I stood in front of it, pointing the Browning at it with my right hand, and with my left bravely swished it to one side. The girl inside jumped and the lilac-blue eyes looked suddenly frightened. I felt foolish and lowered the gun. I said wearily,

"All right, Virgin, you can come out now."

Virginia stepped uncertainly out of the shower cubicle. She was dressed in the blouse and skirt that she had worn for the beach last night, and her whisky-golden hair looked even more beautiful by daylight. She was embarrassed, small in voice and small in stature, and making me feel like a heavy-footed clown. She said awkwardly,

"I'm sorry, Mike. I didn't mean to alarm you — "

I said kindly, "Don't worry about it. If I had been half as alarmed as you are I would have shot through the curtain and looked at you afterwards."

I led her out into the bedroom and she continued her fumbling apologies while I made the Browning safe and stuffed it back into its holster.

"I thought you might have your Nigerian friend with you, he seems to stick pretty close. Or perhaps that police captain who was looking for me. I don't know really. It just seemed best to hide until I was sure you were alone."

"How did you get in?"

"I bribed the maid to let me in, the one who makes the beds on this floor. I told her that I wanted to wait for you and give you a surprise, and she thought — she thought what you thought last night."

I couldn't resist a grin at that. "Virgin, you may get top marks for chastity, but you're not doing your reputation much good."

She smiled faintly, and to put her more at ease I returned the holstered Browning to the dressing-table drawer, and then led her out into the main room. I knew she was nervous of the bed. I made her sit down and when we were both comfortable I said bluntly,

"Now let's get down to business. We both know that you're in trouble. We both know that the police are looking for you. And we both know that the maid was wrong in thinking what I thought last night. There's only one reason for you to be here, and that's because you've changed your mind since last night and decided that you are going to tell me all about whatever is bothering you. So go ahead, I'm listening. Take a deep breath and get it all off your chest."

She nodded not very happily, as though she was making the best out of bad circumstances. She said slowly,

"I'll try and start right from the beginning. That way it will be easier."

I nodded encouragement.

"First, I lied a little when I told you that I was a secretary. I just thought that that was a dull job that wouldn't lead you into asking any more questions. The truth is that I came out to Africa as a teacher. I volunteered to work eighteen months in one of the small village schools in the interior. It was a place called Wanendi, but that's not really important. I've finished my term of duty now, and I enjoyed it. It's like one of those small ideals I told you about. I haven't done anything to change the world, or anything that you would even notice, but some of those little black children I taught might grow up with more hope, and to lead better lives. If some of them have grasped that not every white face is an enemy, then at least that is something.

"But that's just the general background. I left Wanendi two weeks ago, but before I went home I wanted to have a holiday so I stayed on here in Lagos. I had made a few friends, mostly other teachers and people connected with the schools. One was a Nigerian teacher named John Sikuvu. He wanted to show me Lagos, and it was through John that I received an invitation to meet Sir Stanley Okuwa. John's uncle was Chief Seletso who was a close friend of the Premier. We were among the guests at the garden party that Sir Stanley gave three days ago. The day the revolution broke out."

Her face was pale with the memory and her voice dwindled into silence, and I knew that she was telling me the truth. I knew something else too, and that was that Virginia West was potential dynamite. I said quietly,

"Keep going, Virgin, tell me exactly what happened."

She nodded. She sat with her knees pressed together and her hands were a nervous ball in her lap, but she looked into my face as though she felt that I still needed convincing.

"It was not a very large garden party, about a dozen guests altogether. It was at the Premier's home just outside Lagos. He has a lovely big villa with some beautiful lawns and gardens, and lots of shading palms and eucalyptus trees. There were some tables set out on the lawns, with lots of iced orange juice and fruit and things. Chief Seletso introduced John and myself to the Premier. I remember he was very tall and friendly, and asked me questions about the school at Wanendi. I only talked to him for a few minutes, but I liked him very much. Then he was introduced to another guest and John and I had to step back."

She paused, blushing faintly with what I realised a moment later was maidenly modesty.

"It was after we had been there about an hour that I had to find the toilet. It was inside the villa on the upper floor and so I left the garden party for a few minutes. I was very lucky because it was while I was in the toilet that I heard the cars roaring up to the villa, and then a lot of shouting and then shooting. It was a hideous noise. They must have been using machine-guns or something like that. There was a continuous sound of bullets going off, and screaming — the screaming was awful. It was all outside for the first minute, and then I heard more shooting, and things breaking, and the servants screaming inside the villa. They were rushing about below and I knew they were chasing the servants down and killing them.

"I was petrified with fright. I didn't dare go outside to find out what was happening, and I was terrified that if I stayed where I was then someone would smash the door down and drag me out of the toilet. There was a small window and I pushed it wide open. I could see down to the lawns at the back of the house but there was no one there. Everything was happening at the front. Then I heard men running up the stairs and kicking open doors, and somebody was shouting orders in Hausa to search the whole of the top floor. I got out of the window then, standing on the toilet seat so that I could reach up and wriggle through, but first I unbolted the door so that they wouldn't have to break it down and know that somebody had been inside. It was a two-storey drop to the ground, but once I was half out of the window I could reach up and grab the edge of the roof so I pulled myself up that way. I lay flat and listened and I heard someone bang open the door of the toilet beneath me, but they didn't come through to look out of the window. I was glad then that I had thought to unlock the door before I climbed out.

"I must have laid there in a huddle for several minutes, too frightened to move. I could still hear them moving about inside the villa, and I was afraid that they would come up on to the roof. Then the noise quietened down, the shooting and the screaming had stopped and there was just the shouting and the boots tramping about. I heard them running down to ground level again, and that was when I risked moving across the roof to look down on the front lawns where we had been holding the garden patty. It was a complete shambles. There were six Land-Rovers scattered in a wide circle. It looked as though they had charged up the main drive and then swung out across the lawns to make sure that nobody escaped. All the tables were overturned and over half of the guests were lying dead or wounded. There were soldiers in Federal Army uniform moving about everywhere, and they were holding Sir Stanley and about four other men prisoner. One of the other men was Chief Seletso but I didn't know the others. John Sikuvu was one of those who were already dead.

"While I was watching an officer came out of the villa. He was a major, I think, and he seemed to be in charge. He made Okuwa and Seletso and the three other men all line up on the lawn, and then he walked behind them with his revolver and shot all of them one at a time in the back of the head. He murdered them all in cold blood, and yet he was so calm about it, as though they were not really human beings that he was killing at all. It was horrible."

She was visibly trembling now and her face had lost all of its colour. I knew she needed help to go on and so I got up and poured two stiff drinks. I handed her one and she drank carefully, choked a little, and then continued.

"When Okuwa and Seletso and the other three men were dead the major started to go around all the other guests who had fallen. One or two of them must have been wounded but still alive, because he put the gun to the back of their heads and shot them too. I couldn't bear to look any more and I just laid flat and covered my head up with my arms. Then suddenly there was a lot of shouting in the lawns below and everybody started shooting again. I pushed myself up to take another look and I saw that one of the guests was running away. He must have only pretended to be dead at first, and then wriggled away through the shrubs and flower beds beside the lawns. He was another chief named Malundi. I recognised him because he was the only man there who had been wearing an *agbada*, that's one of the long embroidered robes the men often wear over the top of their trousers, the other male guests had all been wearing Western suits. I thought at first that they must hit him, he made such an obvious target and all the soldiers were blazing away with their guns. But he was turning very fast and dodging through the palm trees, and then he jumped over the four-foot wall that runs round the villa grounds. A lot of the troops chased after him but they didn't bring him back so I knew that he had escaped. The major in charge of the troops was in a hurry to get away and he blew a whistle to bring them all back. They all scrambled aboard their Land-Rovers and drove off, but they picked up the body of Sir Stanley Okuwa and carried it away with them.

"I waited about five minutes until they were out of sight and it was all very quiet, and then I made my way down from the roof. The villa looked as though somebody had thrown a bomb inside. All the mirrors and glassware

163

were smashed and the bullets had torn big chunks of plaster out of the walls. All the doors had been left swinging on the hinges and the servants were all in scattered heaps like rag dolls, all dead and bleeding. The smell of blood and the burning powder smell made me feel sick. I ran out into the garden but I stopped to look at John Sikuvu. He had been shot in the chest and he was dead. I didn't look at any of the others because I knew they were dead too. I'm not very brave and I just ran away."

She had finished her drink so I gave her another one. She drank half of that too, and when her hands had steadied I asked her quietly,

"Why haven't you told this to anyone before?"

"Because I didn't know who to trust. The soldiers who attacked the villa wore Federal Army uniform, but I wasn't sure whether they were rebels or whether they were under the command of General Makefa. When I ran away after the attack I managed to find a bus to bring me into Lagos and I came back to my room here at the hotel. I felt sick and ill and I had a splitting headache, I just didn't know what to think or do. All I knew was that I had been a witness to a political murder and that that could be dangerous for me if I made the mistake of telling the wrong people. I finally took six aspirin tablets and knocked myself out for the night. I thought that I could think better with a clear head in the morning.

"I was wrong about that, because although I did wake up with a clear head the whole mess had got more involved. The papers and the radio were full of reports about the revolutionaries taking over Kaduna and Kano in the north, and also about Sir Stanley Okuwa being missing, I couldn't understand that last bit, because I knew that Sir Stanley Okuwa was dead. Chief Malundi had escaped and he must have known that too, and he was a member of the Federal Government and a close friend of General Makefa. His silence made me more confused and cautious. I did think that perhaps Malundi hadn't escaped from the villa as I first believed, but later in the day I saw his photograph in a late edition of the *New Nigerian*. He was entering Government House with some other members of the Federal Cabinet, so I know that he is alive. That was the day they handed the country over to martial law under Makefa.

"I knew that the Government had to be covering up some of the known facts, and so I decided to keep quiet for a little longer. I knew I had to tell my story to somebody, but I didn't know who to tell. Then you appeared at the hotel and I made that silly approach to you last night. I wanted to find out more about you before deciding whether to trust — whether to tell you anything. Then I got all uncertain and mixed-up again when you told me that you were an arms salesman. I thought that you might prefer to see Nigeria have a civil war. You would sell more guns that way."

I said sadly, "Virgin, I only sell guns where wars are unavoidable. There are already enough markets."

She nodded miserably. "Anyway, I slept on it again last night, wondering who else I might approach. Finally I decided that the only thing to do was to go to the British High Commission here in Lagos. It was such an obvious answer that I wondered why I hadn't thought of it before. I was all set to go there this morning, but then I heard that rebel broadcast from Kaduna over the radio. I waited again because I expected Makefa or the Federal Government to make some answer. They did so an hour later, but neither side was telling the truth as I saw it. I had to do all my thinking again, and now I'm sure that the rebel version must be nearer to the truth. If those troops who attacked the villa were not under Makefa's orders, then why are Makefa and Malundi confusing the facts?"

"That's a good question, but what stopped you from taking all this to the High Commission? Why did you change your mind again and come to me?"

"Because I found out that the police are looking for me. I waited all morning in case there were any more broadcasts, and then I came down from my room, intending to go to the High Commission as I had planned. But as I passed through the hotel foyer I saw your army lieutenant friend talking to the police captain in the lounge. They didn't see me, but I overheard enough of their conversation to know that they were discussing me. I hurried out of the hotel but after that I didn't dare go to the British High Commission because I thought that that would be the logical place for the police to watch and pick me up. I felt that I had to get off the streets and so I went into a cinema. It was air-conditioned and quite cool, but I didn't even notice what film was showing. I was just getting more and more worried and I didn't know what to do. When I left the cinema there was nowhere else to go except to try and get back into the hotel to see you."

I said softly, "Virgin, you are in a mess of trouble. Why didn't you grab the next plane out on that first morning after the attack? You could have told your story to the press in London, or anywhere — you would have been safe out of Nigeria."

"But I have to stay in Nigeria." She said it simply as though it was an obvious truth. "Don't you see, Mike, I'm an eye-witness. I can identify that army major who murdered Okuwa and the others. I don't want to run away from it. I just want to be sure that when I tell my story I tell it to the right people."

I smiled a little, sadly again. "Is it that important? Do you really think that you can change anything?"

"Mike, you won't understand!" She leaned forward, pleading with me. "Sir

Stanley Okuwa wasn't just the Premier of the Federal Cabinet, he was also the religious leader of all Nigeria's Moslems. At the moment the Moslems are quiet because they're observing the fast of Ramadan. One of the things they're forbidden during Ramadan is to commit any acts of violence, but once the fast is over there could be terrible bloodshed in Nigeria. The man who murdered Okuwa must be brought to justice before then, and I'm the *only* person who can recognise him!"

This was the second time today that I had heard the ominous threat of that Ramadan deadline, first from Makefa and now from Virginia West. It gave me a shivery feeling along my spine and I made a mental note to check my calendar and be well out of it before the month was up. Meanwhile I had to talk sense to Virginia. I said frankly,

"You're not the only person who can recognise him. There's this Chief Malundi you've told me about, he's an eye-witness too. It's his country so why not leave it to him?"

"Because I think that Malundi may be conspiring with Makefa to hide the truth."

"If that's the case then your chances of proving the truth are very small indeed. And in any case it's unlikely that you will ever see the major who led those troops again."

She said insistently, "But you're wrong, Mike. I have seen him again! I saw him today — here in Lagos. When I came out of that cinema I saw him walking past on the opposite side of the street. He wasn't in uniform, he was wearing a dark blue suit, but I'm sure it was the same man!"

I stared at her, and there was a sudden nasty, jerking sensation in the pit of my stomach. For with the whole of the military on stand-by alert it was unlikely that there were very many army officers wandering around out of uniform, and the civilian suit worn by my good friend Major Sallah was also a dark blue.

10

Cold Snatch

I STOOD up and poured myself a second stiff drink. I needed it to give myself time to think. Virginia had told a long story and now she was glad that it was over. She sat quietly in her chair and seemed to be in no hurry to hear my response. My feelings were mixed. My job was to sell guns, and the basic rule was never to get involved in anything beyond the field of pure business. But now the girl had put me on the spot. It wasn't exactly flattering that she had come to me the second time only as a last resort, but I had to do something to help her. I sat down again and she looked at me expectantly.

I said, "Do you know exactly why Captain Shabani is looking for you?"

"Shabani?" The name meant nothing but she was quick to understand. "You mean the policeman who came to see you earlier today?"

"That's right. What exactly did you overhear between Shabani and Kamau?"

"Not very much really. The police captain referred to me as the white girl who was with you last night. Your lieutenant friend said he didn't know anything about me, except that you and I went to the beach together, and then they both decided to come up to your room and ask you some questions. I ran away then before they came out of the lounge."

She wasn't very helpful, and I asked doubtfully,

"Virgin, are you sure you haven't done anything against the law?"

"I don't think so."

She considered it carefully and shook her head, and I knew it had been a ridiculous question to ask. She would be as pure in mind as she was in body. I said decidedly,

"Then we can assume that Shabani must either know or suspect that you were a guest at Okuwa's last garden party. Perhaps there was a guest list to check against the bodies and he knows that there is one missing." It occurred to me that if there had been a guest list then Shabani would have known her name when he had called on me, but as he could have been simply testing the truth of my replies his professed ignorance need not be significant. I continued my first train of thought aloud.

"Shabani is a police officer, and it's his job to dig out the facts and administer the law. It seems to me that you made a mistake in running away from him. He's probably the very man to whom you should tell your story if you want to see justice done."

"But if there was a guest list then he would know that Malundi had been there too. Why hasn't he questioned Malundi? And why was the Premier's murder covered up for two days when they knew that he was dead?"

"I won't even try and answer that last question, but I'll try the first. Perhaps Shabani has questioned Chief Malundi. Perhaps he merely needs you to confirm or add to the facts. Perhaps he's a genuine, conscientious police officer worried about your safety. I can't imagine any police officer who would willingly allow a murder witness to wander unprotected in your circumstances. And the only way we'll find out for sure is to go and talk to him. I'll come with you if you like, for moral support and to ensure fair play."

"Mike, I'm not sure. Malundi and Makefa represent the Government and the Army, if they're covering something up then why not the police too?"

I smiled wryly. "Virgin, you don't have any faith in anyone. You're beginning to sound like me. What's happened to those small ideals, and the belief that there must be a few

175

honest men in this world of villains?"

She looked at me angrily. "Mike, don't try to sneer at me — not about this, please."

"I'm sorry, I didn't mean it to sound that way." I was sincere about that. "But let's try to be objective. In an involved political situation like this no one can be sure of anything, and if you want to be idealistic and stop a wave of bloodshed at the end of Ramadan then you've got to take some risks. Telling everything to Shabani is at least a justifiable risk."

"But I'm not worried about taking any personal risk. I'm not important. It's what I know and what I saw that is so terribly important."

"You still have to gamble. You could make the wrong move but you must do something. If you won't go to Shabani let me take you right to the top, direct to Makefa. He's the strong man in command, but he needs me. He hasn't yet got his hands on that arms shipment from Trans-Global, and also he's going to need regular follow-up deliveries of ammunition. That's my insurance and I can spread it to cover you too."

"No!" She was loud and definite. "I think that Makefa must have given the orders to kill Okuwa, and if I'm right then there's no possible insurance for either of us. It would be madness to go to Makefa."

I didn't agree there, but I could hardly tell her what I knew about Sallah. At the same time I knew that without telling her I would never persuade her to go to either Makefa or the police. There was only one other alternative and I said bluntly,

"All right, I'll take you to the British High Commission, and even if the police are on the look-out for you I'll guarantee to get you inside. You can tell your story there. They'll probably send for Shabani and you'll have to repeat it to him anyway, but at least you'll have the advice of the High Commissioner first, and diplomatic protection afterwards."

She said uncertainly, "But how can you guarantee to get me inside?"

I answered that by going into the bedroom and returning with the Browning P-35. I pulled it out of the holster for the second time that evening and cocked it in my hand. I said simply,

"The M'Call personal guarantee, but don't worry that I'll try and shoot my way in or anything stupid like that. I'll just point it politely at anyone who steps in our path and ask them to kindly get out of our way. Most people do as they're told when you point guns at them. Heroes are a very scarce commodity in most places, and the odds are that I won't even have to show it at all."

Virginia remained doubtful. The evening had grown late as we talked and darkness had descended outside. She said weakly,

"The High Commission will be closed now."

"This is an emergency. They'll open up when I hammer on the door."

She didn't answer that, and I didn't give her time to find any more arguments. I went back into the bedroom and put on a white shirt and a tie. When I had tucked in the shirt I strapped the holstered Browning around my waist, the gun fitting comfortably just forward of my left hip. I pulled on my jacket and buttoned it up to cover the holster, and then went back to Virginia. She was standing up and waiting, and from somewhere she had retrieved her handbag which I hadn't noticed before. She said reluctantly,

"I suppose you're right. I can't think of anything else."

"Of course I'm right." I did the mental equivalent of crossing my fingers and hoped that I was. "And we'd better go now, before Shabani catches up with you. I didn't help him very much the first time he called, but it's always possible that he'll come back — especially when he learns that you're staying here at this hotel."

She nodded and allowed me to take her arm. I led her out into the corridor and then down the stairs to the foyer, avoiding the lift. She took a step towards the main doors but I held her back.

"Not that way. My lieutenant friend has a nasty habit of watching the main entrance from the lounge. I always go out by the side door when I don't want to be seen."

She looked at me strangely but didn't protest. We used the side door and then circled round to the front of the hotel to pick up her Ford Corsair from the forecourt. I took the wheel again and she sat nervously beside me, glancing back over her shoulder at the hotel. I paused only long enough to ensure that the Browning was pointed down the outside of my thigh, and then I started the car and got moving.

I handled the car with only half my

mind on my driving, the other half was pondering over what Virginia had told me. Once I had handed her over to the British High Commission I would have passed the buck and escaped most of the complications she had brought me, but there would still be a few awkward ones left. Mainly they revolved around Major Sallah. If he was the same man who had murdered Okuwa and his guests then he deserved nothing better than to be handed over to Shabani or Makefa, but the ticklish problem lay in how could I betray him without revealing that I had been attempting to fix a deal with the rebels. Perhaps I could stay clear, and hope that Sallah could be captured without my help, and here an even less noble thought intruded. With luck I might even be able to arrange a deal through Sallah with the Revolutionary Council in Kaduna before Sallah was captured. That would be the best of all possible worlds; a large sale to both sides, the Premier's murderer brought to justice and the arms made unnecessary, and then I could step in again to re-buy the arms cheap for another resale elsewhere. I could also end up shot in the head somewhere along the line, and it would all need a lot of careful thought.

We were over the bridge then, and Virginia said suddenly,

"Mike, we're being followed!"

I postponed my thinking and looked back. There were headlights trailing up the street behind us, and despite the dazzle I could recognise the shape of a black Jaguar. Kamau must have got wise to my evasive tactics, but I didn't stop to wonder why he had his headlights on full. I said wryly,

"It's only my lieutenant friend, he gets sharper all the time. But I don't think he'll interfere, his job is only to watch me and report."

Virginia wasn't reassured. She kept looking back and we were still five minutes away from sanctuary at the High Commission when she exclaimed,

"Mike, he's getting closer — he's coming past!"

I twisted my head round as the Jaguar roared level, and abruptly I realised that Kamau didn't have an option on all the black Jaguars in Lagos. This was a completely different Jaguar, but it had probably been chosen so that I would think that it was Kamau behind me. The headlights had been full and blinding to prevent me from seeing that there were four heads inside the car instead of just one, and none of them belonged to my trusty watchdog. All this tumbled fast through my waking brain, but the driver of the Jaguar was faster.

The car cut in front of me, forcing me to swing hard left, and then it was braking hard. I had to brake hard too but even so the bonnet of the Corsair crunched into the flank of the Jaguar and was flung even further left. Our wheels mounted the pavement and Virginia screamed and covered her face. The Corsair slammed broadside into a cheap shopfront and a plate glass window collapsed over the roof and the bonnet. The car skidded along the pavement for another two yards and then ended with a sickening crunch against the shop doorway. The windscreen cracked and frosted in front of me but mercifully it didn't shatter, and in the same moment the back end of the Corsair slewed out into the road again before coming to a final rest.

Virginia was shaken and white with fright, although she didn't look otherwise hurt, but I was fighting mad. I shoved open my door and started to push my way out, and then I saw that the Jaguar had also stopped and that the four men from inside were bearing down on me fast. They were four determined black faces and they weren't hurrying to apologise or help clear up the mess. The levelled revolvers they carried made that plain. Their leader wore a dark blue suit and I recognised Sallah.

I was beginning to understand and I made a grab for the Browning. I got it clear of the holster but I didn't get a chance to pull the trigger. A revolver barrel cracked down with deft precision across the back of my wrist, and the Browning went spinning into the gutter. I let out a howling curse and from inside the wrecked Corsair Virginia emitted another scream. Then I had my back against the car trying to wrestle four men at once.

The street was miraculously empty. The civilian population had wisely fled and there was no sign of the armed Federal troops who had patrolled in such vast numbers during the past few days. Like policemen they were never visible when they were really needed. With one wrist practically broken I quickly lost the rest of the fight, and with my arms twisted up behind me I was being hustled towards the Jaguar when another car screamed to a violent stop in the darkened street behind us.

The three men holding me stopped and we all managed to look around. It was another black Jaguar and this time it was Kamau who tumbled out. He started forward at a run, pulling at the revolver at his hip, but the effort was as brave as it was hopeless. Sallah had stayed back to drag Virginia out of the Corsair, and although he wanted me alive he had no scruples about killing my faithful lieutenant. I saw him raise his revolver quite calmly, his arm extended straight, and fire. Kamau tumbled round in a clumsy somersault and dropped, his own weapon clattering out of his fingers and his peaked cap rolling down the street. He lay there unwanted and unheeded and I struggled savagely as my three captors resumed our hasty progress to their car. I heard Virginia screaming again, but then someone decided to clout me hard over the head with a revolver barrel and I saw nothing but stars.

I did become aware again when the car was moving. I was stuffed into the back seat, my jacket had been drawn back from my right shoulder, and a hand was ripping at my shirt. I tried to tell Sallah that this is all bloody stupid and unnecessary, but then they had bared my upper arm and I felt a needle go in. There were no stars that time, just a drowning sensation in a whirlpool of blackness.

11

Stark Terror

WE were airborne when I came round for the second time. I recognised the feeling and the faint droning sound of twin engines. I made a cautious effort to open my eyes but they seemed to be glued together, and my eyelashes dragged apart slowly to give me temporarily blurred vision. We were flying in a small, six-seater business aircraft, the cabin only dimly lit, and I had a weird feeling of isolation as though we were suspended in space. There was one seat in front of mine, but beyond that, through the centre aisle, was an outline view of the pilot's back and shoulders, blotting out part of the glowing control panels in the cockpit. He sat motionless, and I could imagine that time and sound had stopped, and that the engine drone was taking place inside my head.

Then the aircraft bumped in an air pocket and I knew that it was real. I looked to my right and saw Virginia huddled in the seat opposite. She was awake but silent and scared, and looked as though her wits were still fuddled. I wondered vaguely why they had bothered to bring her along, but my own mind was too dull to think clearly. Some instinct unrelated to my thoughts made me move my hands and feet, and I was surprised to find that they were free and not tied. Then I wondered why I was surprised. There was nothing that I could do anyway. The plane was flying high in the sky and there would be nothing but swamps and jungle underneath. It was dark beyond the cabin window to my left, but no matter which way we were flying the terrain would be the same. Nigeria was all swamps and jungle; there was nothing else until the deserts of the far north.

I turned my head slowly, looking for Sallah. Two of his tough colleagues who had crewed the Jaguar occupied the first two seats in the cabin, and the third man was relaxed behind Virginia. They were all negro heavyweights, and I learned later that they were all sergeants in the Federal Army. I had to shift my weight as I twisted my neck further round, and the sound made all three of them look sharply towards me. I could sense their movement and their stares. Sallah sat immediately behind me, still looking unruffled in his dark blue suit, and again wearing his polite black smile. His teeth gleamed faintly in the gloom.

My vision was still hazy, but there was an ache in the back of my skull, and there were spasms of nausea swimming like circling goldfish through my stomach, but my voice came through clearly and precisely.

"Major Sallah, you're a fool."

His shoulders moved in a casual apology.

"Perhaps."

"This won't get you anywhere, you must know that. If you've done anything, you've made it impossible for me to help you."

His smile appeared to contain genuine regret.

"I am sorry, Major M'Call, but I am under orders. Major-General Karagwe has become impatient with my efforts in Lagos. He demands instead that you be brought to him in Kaduna."

"But I can do nothing from Kaduna!"

"You were doing nothing in Lagos."

"You're wrong! I was doing plenty in Lagos. I told you an official deal with Trans-Global was out, but I cabled every private contact I knew to find out what other stocks were available. That's why I told you two days. I have to wait for the answers to comeback."

Sallah frowned. "You should have told me these details when we met earlier today. I made my report by radio immediately afterwards, and if I had been able to include these facts then perhaps I would not have been instructed to bring you north for a personal interview. At least I could have questioned the order and advised against it. Now it is too late, we have already flown past the point of no return."

I wanted to argue with him, but my head ached and I knew it would be of no use. The twist in my neck was uncomfortable and those sickly goldfish were now making rolling dives through the loose, watery sensation that was my stomach. I turned away to face front and as I did so I found Virginia's lilac-blue eyes fixed upon me in a shocked stare. Her face was a pale mask of betrayed horror, and I realised that she had heard and understood every word.

And there was something else. There was a deeper fear that was not part of the knowledge that I had been contemplating a deal with the rebels, or even the fact of being kidnapped. My mind was slow, but then those dark blue eyes flickered past me towards Sallah, and then closed quickly with a little spasm of shuddering as she looked away. I understood then and I prayed that she would keep her head, stay calm, and keep her mouth shut. There was no longer any doubt that Sallah was the army major who had led the assault upon Sir Stanley Okuwa's villa, and the massacre of its inhabitants. Virginia had recognised him again, but obviously, and mercifully, he was not yet aware that she had been a witness from the villa roof. As long as he remained ignorant of that fact we stood a reasonable chance of being returned to Lagos, but if Virginia panicked and revealed what she knew then neither of us would be returned anywhere except to a hole in the ground.

The thought made me sweat.

★ ★ ★

The sky began to lighten and dawn was a blazing array of colour charging in from the west. Most of it was red, like blood, and it didn't make me feel any better at all. Below us was one vast forest, just as I had expected, rumpled like a thick green blanket. On top it was all fresh, sparkling leaf and foliage, but underneath it would be black and steamy, tangled and rotting. Many dark, nocturnal happenings would occur under that blanket, but all in cruelty and hunger, and never love. I reflected then that if the jungle knew no compassion, at least it also knew no power-lust and no hate, and I couldn't help wondering whether perhaps the beasts inhabited a better world than mankind.

An hour later we landed at a small airfield just outside Kaduna. It was a smooth landing, and when we got out I noted that the plane was a Beagle B.206. It carried civilian registration markings and I guessed that it had been commandeered during the rebel takeover. Its legal owners had probably been jailed or shot, depending upon how much resistance they had made. Sallah had explained how the plane had picked us up from a hard sand beach west of Lagos, and I wondered whether Okuwa's body had been freighted north in the same way. The Premier had never been found and it seemed a likely possibility.

The worst effects of the dope had worn off by the time we arrived, although I had to steady Virginia and help her down on to the runway. I moved first to forestall anybody else from using the opportunity to paw her, but she quickly pushed me away as though she didn't much want to be touched by me either. She had not yet spoken a word, and neither had her face regained any colour. The sun was already strong, and as we stood blinking she moved apart from me as though I was no better than Sallah and his bunch of thugs. There was nothing that I could do except curse inwardly and wish that I had had the sense to let the fog clear from my brain before

I had started arguing with Sallah and opening my big fat mouth.

There was a strong escort to meet us, five jeeps filled with soldiers and commanded by a young lieutenant. They churned up a smokescreen of dust as they drew up beside the plane and the lieutenant and Sallah swapped salutes. The lieutenant had a clean white smile that made me think of Kamau, and I had to hold back the urge to reach out and break Sallah's neck in my hands. Virginia and I were shoved into the back of the leading jeep, and Sallah ousted the lieutenant from his seat beside the driver, allowing him to cling on to the running board instead. Then the whole convoy wheeled round and we were carried at racing speed into Kaduna.

It was a nightmare drive. The reports that reached Lagos had said that when the rebels seized Kaduna they had promptly murdered the Northern Regional Premier, the local Army Brigade Commander, his wife, and three or four loyal colonels, but obviously they hadn't bothered to stop there. The dusty streets were a shambles of looted shops, overturned cars and butchered corpses. A burned-out jeep had been pushed to one side of the road just beyond the airfield, a skeleton picked clean by fire and flame instead of the hooked beaks of the distant vultures. Further along a small truck had crashed into the bole of a palm tree, covering itself with a funeral shroud of fallen green fronds. The driver was still crushed dead behind the wheel. Probably he had been run off the road by speeding army vehicles in the heat of the moment, but nobody had bothered to move him yet. In the city the hot sun broiled the stink of blood and death and refuse in the gutters, and stray dogs sniffed at the strung-out victims of the revolt. There were black soldiers everywhere, grinning cheerfully and wandering, apparently uncontrolled, with rifles and submachine-guns slung across their shoulders. It was disconcerting to see that they wore the same Federal Army uniforms that had been so familiar in Lagos, and there was a sense of lawlessness about them that made me glad that we had been given a strong escort. They stared as we went past, backing away from the speeding jeeps and the swirling dust.

Virginia could feel their eyes, stripping off her clothes despite the swiftness with which we drove by, and despite herself she pressed closer to my side. So far she had kept her nerve but I hadn't stopped sweating. She jumped noticeably when Sallah looked round and said,

"I must apologise for the mess in the streets, but it is impossible to completely restrain the common soldiery in their hour of victory. Nigeria is still Africa and there is much room for improvement. Please do not think of us too badly."

Neither of us answered him, and after a moment he turned away. He seemed genuinely disappointed that I had made no response, as though he had expected me to understand that the bright, shiny omelette of New Nigeria could not be achieved without a few broken eggs. Perhaps he was right, but here all the egg yolks were blood.

A few minutes later we stopped with a squeal of brakes and a crash of gears outside a large, modern hotel in the centre of the city. I noted the name Impala Hotel, but I was mostly impressed by the armed sentries and the piled sandbags that guarded the entrance. The place was fortified to hold off another army. The rest of the convoy skidded to a stop behind us and Virginia and I were ordered out of the jeep and marched into the hotel. Sallah walked beside us and explained briefly,

"This building now serves as the headquarters for the Revolutionary Council. We found it more comfortable than the barracks."

The escort lieutenant led the way

inside and we were met by two more army officers bearing the rank tabs of captain and lieutenant-colonel. There was a brief discussion in Hausa, and then the two officers smiled at me as Sallah made polite introductions. African names are easy to forget unless they're important, and these two I didn't even try to remember. The lieutenant-colonel thanked me for coming in perfect English, and I thanked him for the invitation in perfect sarcasm. If he was offended he didn't show it but simply smiled some more. The captain shouted briskly at the one-pip lieutenant who had met us at the airfield, and then we were on the move again, the lieutenant leading the way upstairs. The lift was apparently not working and neither, judging by the sticky heat, was the air conditioning.

We were taken to a second floor room and Virginia and I were ushered inside. Sallah came in behind us and explained that Major-General Karagwe would wish to see me as soon as he was available, and that meanwhile this would be our room for the duration of our stay. Unless, he added, we preferred separate rooms.

I didn't let Virginia answer that, but told him that the one double room was quite all right. Virginia might not want to share a room with me, but I knew she would be a whole lot safer than if she was on her own. Perhaps she realised that too for she didn't argue. Sallah smiled knowingly, indicated that there was a bathroom across the corridor if we needed it, bowed himself out, and left. He didn't mention it but I guessed that there would also be a guard in the corridor.

When we were alone I surveyed the room. It contained a large double bed, two chairs, a dressing-table and a wardrobe, adequate but totally impersonal. Virginia had kept her back to me and moved away to the window, staring down through the slatted blind. She didn't seem to care that there was only one bed, or seem to expect that

I would offer to be a gentleman and restrict myself to the chairs. She was like a dulled shell of herself, with all hope and feeling drained out.

I moved beside her but she wouldn't look at me. Down below the street was deserted, baked and dusty, but the windows of the shops opposite had been smashed and emptied. From the front of the hotel came the sound of voices, and the revving of an engine. More muted from the distance were fainter shouts, hoarse laughter, and the tinkle of more breaking glass.

We stood for a minute but she didn't speak, and then I put my hands on her shoulders and turned her to face me. I said grimly,

"Snap out of it, Virgin. Curse me, use your claws, kick me, but for Christ's sake do something. You think I've let you down badly and maybe I have, but don't close up on me and brood, get it out of your system."

She wouldn't look up into my eyes, instead she just shook her shoulders away from my hands and then moved round to the other side of the bed. I didn't follow her because I didn't want to hold her forcibly and there was no point in both of us continuously trailing back and forth across the room.

I said wearily, "All right, so I *was* trying to fix up a deal with the rebels, but that was before I knew all the facts. And the rest of this mess isn't my fault at all. How could I know that Sallah would be stupid enough to pull a stunt like this? And it was just sheer bad luck that you happened to get caught up with me!"

She still refused to turn her head, but at least she spoke.

"Are you still going to sell guns to the rebels?"

"I may have to — if it's at all possible I'm not in a particularly good position to refuse." I paused and added, "Especially with you here. You're the lever to help put pressure on me, that's why you were brought along. Sallah isn't aware that you've seen him before, otherwise you'd be dead by now, so there's no other answer."

She looked at me then, and her mouth curled bitterly.

"Don't use me as an excuse, Mister M'Call. Don't pretend that you'll only sell them arms to protect me. We both know that that isn't true, and even if it was I wouldn't want it."

She sat down on the far side of the bed and laid back, closing her eyes to indicate that the conversation was over. She had nothing more to say, but at least I had got some response and I was able to relax. She was scared white but there was still a lot of stubborn courage inside her and I didn't think now that she would crack, that was something to be thankful for. There was a part of me that wanted to go over to the bed and comfort her, but I knew that she wouldn't accept it. So I turned away and stared down through the window, seeing nothing and trying to calculate all the odds and angles. The sweat rolled slowly down my face and I was conscious of a violent thirst. I just couldn't make up my mind whether I needed a long one for my parched throat, or a strong one for my shaky nerves.

12

Strongman Two

AN hour passed, and then there was a polite knock on the door. I walked across and opened it and Sallah stood there with a two-man escort. He had changed out of his blue suit but looked equally smart in his army uniform, complete with peaked cap, revolver holster, and major's tabs on his shoulders. This was how Virginia had seen him before, and I blocked his view to the bed where her face had shown recoil and revulsion. He didn't look past me but simply said,

"Major-General Karagwe has returned. He will speak with you now, Major M'Call."

"Thank you, Major Sallah."

I was trying hard to offend him, but he was trying hard not to notice. He smiled and stood back and I followed him into the corridor. Virginia turned her back on us all, and Sallah shrugged apologetically as he closed the door and sealed her from my view. I noted that there was an armed sentry standing further along the corridor and hoped that he could he trusted. Then I was marched away.

The hotel had a small, private dining-room on the ground floor, separate from the main restaurant and probably reserved for special parties and functions. It contained a single large, oval-shaped table, big enough to seat a dozen people, and they had turned it into a conference room. Half a dozen army officers were ranged around the far side of the table, like judges at a court martial. They included the officers who had greeted our arrival at the hotel, another lieutenant-colonel, two more majors and in the centre Major-General Karagwe. The rebel leader was the only man of that rank present, and I recognised his blunt Negro features, distinguished by a bristly bush of beard, from the photographs that had been circulated in the Lagos press.

There were two more armed soldiers by the door, and our own escort stayed back as Sallah and I went inside. Sallah came to attention and saluted smartly, and the Revolutionary Council saluted briefly in return. The only man who didn't salute was me, but I was here under protest. Sallah and I were both invited to sit down, and we both did so. I kept my eyes on Karagwe as the only one really worth my time and got my piece in first.

"I hope Major Sallah has informed you that bringing me here was a mistake. You want to purchase arms but I can do less for you here than I could in Lagos. If you want to do business then I can only suggest that you return Miss West and myself to Lagos immediately."

It was a nice little speech, but the reaction was dead silence, as though they were all startled that I should have the nerve to start the proceedings out of turn. Karagwe stared at me as though he had been presented with a freak, but then suddenly he began to smile. I was an obscure joke but he was able to see the funny side. The sign was sufficient and his brother officers began to grin. One of the lieutenant-colonels murmured something wryly in Hausa, and Karagwe slapped the table with the palm of his hand and laughed. Then he composed himself more politely to speak to me.

"Major M'Call, you were asked to come here because I thought it would be more simple to talk business direct. I'm sure that we can discuss matters more easily by cutting out the middleman."

I said bluntly, "General, I wasn't asked to come anywhere. I was knocked over the head, drugged, and flown here against my will. I'm not prepared to discuss anything under these conditions."

Karagwe studied me sombrely for a

moment, and then looked ominously towards Sallah.

"Perhaps Major Sallah misinterpreted his instructions. If this is so then he will be severely reprimanded."

Sallah managed to look chastened, but I had seen better acts at an amateur music hall. I knew it wasn't worth pushing and at least they didn't insult me by lingering with the scene. Karagwe returned his gaze to me and continued,

"If there has been any inconvenience then you have our most sincere apologies, but now that you are here I think you must agree that we should take this opportunity to discuss the arms deal that Major Sallah attempted to arrange. We know that Trans-Global Arms, the company which you represent, has agreed to supply General Makefa and the Federal Government with a large shipment of arms and armoured cars for the purpose of crushing down our revolution. We too wish to buy arms and armoured cars, and I can assure you that we can pay the same price, and in the same currency as the Federal Government. Are you prepared to deal with us, or not?"

He made it sound like an ultimatum and I could feel the sweat running down the length of my spine. Most of it was caused by the lack of air conditioning but not all.

I said flatly, "I've already explained to Major Sallah that there is no hope of any kind of a deal with Trans-Global. We're a legal British company, and all arms transactions from Britain require the written approval of the British Government. In your case we wouldn't get it. The question of whether we would be prepared to deal with you doesn't enter into it, the fact is that it isn't possible."

"It is always possible."

"Not in this case."

"You are in business to sell arms. That is your job. There must be a way."

"Not with Trans-Global."

We glared at each other and Karagwe scowled through his beard.

"If it is a question of delivery then we could collect from practically any part of Africa. You would not have to take the risk of shipping directly to Nigeria."

"But it isn't a question of shipping into Africa. It's a matter of getting a permit to ship the arms out of England. The British Government regulations make a brick wall, and there's no way round it. Trans-Global cannot help you."

It was impasse, and we were both losing patience with each other. Karagwe tried to stare through to the back of my head so that he could decide whether I was speaking the truth or just trying to be awkward. Then he said abruptly,

"If you cannot supply arms to us, then you must halt the supply to Makefa!"

That stopped me for a minute, but he was serious. I spread my hands to denote helplessness and said,

"That's equally impossible. Contracts have been signed, clearance papers given, and the arms are already on their way. The shipment is somewhere between Freetown and Lagos aboard the *African Rose*, and there's nothing that I can do to turn her back. She'll dock in two days time."

Karagwe clenched both hands in one massive, black-knuckled club and crashed them down heavily on the table.

"Major M'Call, you are being deliberately unhelpful. You do not seem to realise the seriousness of your position."

I sweated some more and said frankly,

"General, I fully realise the seriousness of my position. I'm a prisoner here and you can have me put up against a wall and shot, or anything else you may consider appropriate. But there's nothing that I can do about it. I can't promise you a supply of arms from Trans-Global because I know it wouldn't be allowed. And I can't promise you that I'll stop the supply of arms from Trans-Global to Makefa because I haven't got the power."

"You could cable your company in London. The cable can be sent from Kaduna."

"They wouldn't listen to me."

"You can explain the seriousness of your position."

"It'll make no difference. I'm only a salesman, I can be replaced. And you can't blackmail Trans-Global."

"There is always the girl."

"All right, shoot the girl. Rape the girl. It changes nothing."

Karagwe was no longer certain about me at all. Perhaps he too had thought that there was an officer and a gentleman inside me. He said at last,

"The girl means nothing to you?"

I said wearily, "That's not the point. It doesn't matter how you treat me, or the girl, there's nothing that I could say or do to influence my company in your favour. That's what I'm trying to get across."

Karagwe tightened his lips, and the gesture flared his thick nostrils into an ugly grimace. He unclenched his hands and drew back from the table, turning to talk in Hausa to the lieutenant-colonel on his left. They all listened attentively, and then Sallah interrupted, speaking quickly in the same language. They all listened to him and then Karagwe looked back to me.

"Major Sallah tells us that you were trying to arrange some kind of a private deal. Explain please."

I didn't know whether to be grateful to Sallah or not. Apart from my personal dislike of dealing under pressure, Virginia had touched a raw nerve in my conscience and I wasn't sure that I wanted to deal with these people at all. Now, however, I had no choice but to go through the motions. Reluctantly I explained.

"I've told you that you won't get

any official shipments, not straight from the factory. But there are second-hand stocks continuously shifting from place to place around the world. For example, a shipment might be sold in the Caribbean to arm a revolution. When it's over the losing side surrenders its arms, the winning side makes an extra profit on selling the surplus. That shipment will return to an arms dealer to be sold again, perhaps in Africa or the Middle East. The same pattern takes place. When the war is over there's a winning side and a losing side. The losers surrender their arms, and the winners sell the surplus back to an arms dealer. The dealer ships them somewhere else again. It goes on and on. Some guns pass through a score of hands, and see service in every corner of the world. I've cabled three private dealers who specialise in such transactions, and I was waiting in Lagos for their replies. If they have any large stocks that can be moved then I might be able to help you."

Karagwe was less hostile, but he was still frowning.

"Might is a vague word, Major M'Call — and we do not particularly desire second-hand weapons. We prefer new, modern weapons to match Makefa's Belgian F.A.L. rifles."

I shrugged. "Then I can only suggest you try the Russians or the Chinese. You won't get factory-new weapons to overthrow a Commonwealth Government from the West."

Karagwe hesitated, and then conferred again with the two lieutenant-colonels. One of the majors put in a tentative word and the captain tried to adjust a facial expression of agreement with them all. I guessed that they all understood English, but they preferred to talk Hausa so that I should not understand them. I seemed to have some doubts on my side so I pressed on at the first pause.

"Gentlemen, I can only help you by putting you in contact with a private dealer. And I can't even do that while

217

you keep me here in Kaduna. I have to be in Lagos to receive and answer those cables. It's to our mutual advantage if you allow me to return."

Karagwe listened to my appeal, and then began to scratch at his jaw through the wiry black strands of his beard. He leaned forward again but his words were still in Hausa and he addressed Sallah at my side. The major answered crisply, gave a few affirmative nods to further questions, and then Karagwe looked back to me and smiled.

"You are aware, I think, that we are still in radio contact with Lagos. We have a few loyal friends there who make it their business to keep us informed of any new Government moves. Major Sallah assures me that it will not be impossible for them to discover the contents of any cables delivered to you at the Ambassadors Hotel. He will take the necessary steps to request this information, and when we are informed of the replies to your cables, then we will decide what to do next."

My feelings towards helpful Major Sallah were growing blacker by the hour, blacker than his own black soul, but there was nothing I could do about it. Karagwe went on,

"While we wait both yourself and the young lady will remain in Kaduna as our guests. You will be confined to the hotel for your own safety, but Major Sallah will provide anything that is needed for your comfort." He stood up to signify that the interview was over, but before he walked out he added a bleak warning, "There may be no acceptable outcome to this delay, so I would advise you to spend your waiting time in trying to devise some other alternative — something that would again be to our mutual advantage."

★ ★ ★

The same two soldiers marched me smartly back to my second-floor prison, accompanied again by Sallah who was of the opinion that I should at least try to appear more helpful before the major-general. Presumably a more humble attitude was desired on my part, but I failed to listen to him very closely. The conference room had been situated deep inside the hotel and remote from any outside noises, but now that we were approaching the outer wing I could hear the echoes of a disturbance in the street.

The mixed sounds of laughter and screaming must have been very commonplace in Kaduna, for Sallah barely seemed to notice. I quickened my pace and only then did he stop talking and pay attention. The screaming continued, a woman's broken wailing rising to a series of urgent shrieks. It was the clearest sound above a whole confusion of shouts and cries and already I was running. Right then I didn't care about the armed soldiers behind me, but fortunately Sallah chose to run at my side and they refrained from shooting.

The sentry was still standing outside

the room where I had left Virginia and I flung him roughly out of the way. I yanked open the door and burst in, and then stopped. Sallah jolted against my shoulder and I didn't realise until later that he had already drawn his revolver. Virginia was alone and unharmed, standing at the window with her back towards us, her hands clenched tight through the slats of the blind. She was staring down into the street where the screaming had stopped but the laughter was still taking place, and I went quickly to her side.

There were over a dozen black soldiers laughing and squabbling in the dust. They were gleeful and aggressive, staggering and rolling in a drunken stupor. They made a squirming heap of black bodies, draped with weapons and scraps of army clothing, and beneath them was the body of a white woman, naked but now mercifully still and silent, like a soiled dummy from a tailor's window. She had pale yellow hair and her face was bruised and

221

bleeding. The biggest of the soldiers succeeded in his attempts to mount her, thrusting away his arguing companions who were trying to take his place.

Sallah was behind me and I turned on him harshly.

"For God's sake do something useful! Get down there and stop them!"

He looked surprised and I shouted angrily.

"They're your troops! You're supposed to be an officer! Get down there and control them!"

He nodded abruptly and then turned and hurried out, slamming the door behind him. In the same moment there was a fresh burst of noise and shouting from below as one of the lieutenant-colonels came running round the corner of the hotel to restore order. He led a squad of sober soldiery and carried his pistol at the ready. He didn't hesitate to shoot the big soldier who was committing rape squarely in the back, and the group beneath us began to scatter. I had no desire to watch any more and turned to Virginia.

She had stopped watching long ago, her eyes were shut tight and she clung to the slats of the blind crucified by fear. Her face was whiter than I would have believed possible in any live human being.

I had difficulty in unlocking her hands from the plastic slats of the blinds, and when I succeeded I noted that the sharp edges had cut deep red grooves across her palms. I pulled her away from the window and she stumbled with her face against my chest. I had to hold her up and said as softly as I could,

"It's over, Virgin. I think the woman is dead, so she can't suffer any more."

From the street came the sounds of shouts and more shots, and I closed my hands over her ears. When the commotion quietened a little she looked up and opened her eyes. Her mouth trembled and then she said,

"It was awful, Mike. They chased her down the street and caught her . . . They were drunk and laughing and she was screaming . . . They tore all her clothes off while she screamed . . . They — they were like wild children tearing the wings off a live bird . . . "

I said quietly, "I can imagine. This is much of Africa's problem, away from the cities and universities so many of them are still children. They'll mature given time. Africa will outgrow its Congoes and its Nigerias, or at least space them out with bright patches like the rest of the world; but first it has to pass through adolescence."

They were the kind of words with which she might have tried to convince me, but Virginia wasn't listening. Instead she was violently sick down the front of my shirt.

13

Time Wasted

THE fuss died down and the street emptied. Sallah came back later and seemed puzzled to find that I had stripped to the waist and washed my shirt. It was then hanging on the back of a chair to dry. He explained that the rioting soldiers we had seen had looted a previously undiscovered beer cellar, and made it sound as though their only crime lay in getting drunk on a late spree instead of releasing their high spirits in the initial wave of looting some three days previously. The woman, he added, was the wife of the French manager of a small factory that had produced groundnut oil nearby. Her husband had been killed during the rebel takeover, and she had been foolish enough to

225

elude the guards responsible for her protection. He made that sound as though her fate was all her own fault, and it wasn't until I pressed him on the point that he regretfully admitted that she was dead.

He was as polite as ever as he apologised to Virginia for the unfortunate scene she had been obliged to witness, and assured us both that it could not happen again. Virginia made no response, sitting quietly on the edge of the bed and refusing to look at him. I intervened and asked him to leave, for I was worried that he would press her and prompt an outburst that would condemn us both. Sallah shrugged and went out.

The rest of the day passed in sweating confinement. My shirt dried in twenty minutes but I didn't bother to put it on again. Virginia lay dully on the bed, never speaking, while I either stood by the window or sat on one of the chairs. The guard brought us two glasses and a large jug of cold water that quickly became tepid, and later a meal of unappetising vegetable stew that contained no meat. I ate but Virginia didn't. The flies were the only things that bothered us through the long, hot afternoon. Kaduna was quiet, just occasional voices, and the occasional sound of an engine. I hoped that the cables I had sent from Lagos would yield something positive, but I took Karagwe's advice and brooded on what I could possibly do about it if they were not.

The day wore out. Beyond the slatted window blind the glare faded and the street filled with long shadows. Our room darkened, but mercifully became something less than an oven full of African heat. Virginia stirred, finding the energy to get up from the bed and pour herself a glass of lukewarm water. It was only the third time she had moved throughout the day, and each time for the same purpose. The back of her blouse was a big wet patch that spread across both shoulders. She sipped her water slowly, reluctant to go near the window, and outside I heard a jeep pull up in front of the hotel and stop. I stopped watching her and didn't realise that she had turned to look at me. She asked in a low voice,

"Mike, are you sincere about not wanting to do a deal with the rebels?"

She had asked something similar before my interview with Karagwe, but this time it was unexpected. I had explained our position after Sallah had left us for the second time, leaving nothing out and telling her the full details about those cables for spares and my hopes that I could eventually bluff or talk my way into a return trip to Lagos, but she had made no comment then. Now it was apparent that she had not been in a shocked coma as I had believed, but had been giving the matter a whole lot of thought, to be more precise somewhere between six and seven hours of thought.

I said warily, "I won't deal with them if I can avoid it — not after this."

I could have added that it would be bad for trade to allow myself to be blackmailed in any way, but it was more tactful to let that remain unsaid. Virginia twisted her lips bitterly.

"You mean that you will deal with them if you can't wriggle out of it?"

I didn't like the word wriggle, but we were talking and I didn't want to make any backward steps. I nodded cautiously and said,

"That's one way of putting it. I might have to go as far as putting them in touch with a private dealer in order to get us off the hook, but it isn't worth becoming a martyr to refuse. They're determined and they'll eventually get in touch with the right people anyway."

"But if they're delayed long enough perhaps the Government can bring them under control before they get the extra arms to create a lot of bloodshed."

"Perhaps, but I thought you didn't trust Makefa, or the Government either."

"That was before I knew for certain that it was the rebels, and your friend Major Sallah, who murdered Okuwa and all the others."

She was getting heated and I had to touch a hasty finger to my lips.

"Easy now, keep your voice down. Talk like that can get us both killed if it's loud enough to be overheard."

I paused and looked into her eyes, finding them unnervingly searching and steady. She had come alive again, vanquishing the numbing effects of her fear, and I asked with foreboding,

"What do you expect me to do?"

"We must escape."

She said it simply, as though we were hero prisoners of war with a firm duty towards King and country. I responded gently.

"Virgin, that's not a very sensible idea."

"Perhaps not. But these people are not fools. They won't let you get away without making some definite deal to supply them with arms. The only real way for you to get out of here without doing that is to escape."

I said just as gently, "It isn't possible."

She shook her head in definite disagreement.

"It is possible, Mike. I've been listening to the sound of the jeeps that keep coming up to the front of the hotel. The last one to arrive is still there, and I'm sure there's another one besides. When it gets dark we could make an attempt at getting out through the window, and then try to steal a jeep. The rainy season hasn't started yet so the roads should be good between here and Lagos. If we can get out of Kaduna then we stand a chance."

She made it sound easy but the prospect didn't tempt me at all. Already I could see looming problems. Six hundred miles of jungle roads was one, patrol difficulties was another, rebel pursuit and rebel ambush tied for third place, and these would not even start until we had broken out of Kaduna. I gestured quietly to the window and asked,

"Do you really want to climb down into *that* street?"

She knew what I meant but she had weighed that possibility too. She said firmly,

"I'll take that risk. It's only important that I get back to Lagos to tell them what I know — but I need a man to help me."

★ ★ ★

I tried to talk her out of it, but I had no success. I couldn't get tough with her and I couldn't even argue too loudly. With her knowledge she was still dynamite, and had to be handled with the smoothest of velvet gloves. I felt that if I didn't adopt her plans then she would have no trust in me at all, and then the peak of courage and determination that she had built up would seep away. There's a narrow and oft-quoted borderline between genius and madness, and Virginia was on a parallel borderline between heroism and despair. If I allowed her to collapse it could be complete, and then she might do something really stupid, like losing her head, cursing me and accusing Sallah all in the same burst of hysteria. Every moment that we were held captive there was that risk.

It was dark when I made my final surrender, and she had just pressed home the point that the two jeeps were still parked at the front of the hotel. We had not yet heard them drive away. I said at last,

"All right, we'll try it — but I'm not going out of that window with nothing but my bare hands. The guard in the corridor is carrying a submachine-gun, and that's what we'll need to give ourselves some covering fire when we grab the jeep. You'll have to help me to get that gun before we leave."

She hesitated. We hadn't bothered to switch on the light and her face was just a dim blur in the gloom. Then she asked,

"How can I help you?"

I gave it some thought and then said,

"The bathroom is just across the corridor. Go there, but leave the door slightly open. Take off your blouse to wash and give the guard some kind of peep show. And leave this door slightly open too. If you can distract him then I can do the rest."

She nodded, and I knew she wasn't allowing herself time to think about it.

"When?"

I was the one who hesitated, but the iron was hot for both of us. If we were to try at all there was only one answer.

"Now."

She nodded again, and then turned and walked to the door. I followed her and pressed my back flat against the wall. We both listened for a moment, but heard nothing. Then she stretched out her hand and I saw that it was trembling before her fingers steadied around the doorknob. She twisted and drew the door open, and a sharp beam of light fell like a bright wall between us. I drew my shoulders back even tighter against the wall, holding my breath in the dark shadow, and then she walked out into the lighted corridor.

She pulled the door to behind her, but left a small three-inch gap. Through it I saw the armed soldier standing two yards away down the corridor. It wasn't the same man who had been there this morning, but he carried an identical submachine-gun slung across his shoulder, and that was all that mattered. He watched with interest as Virginia went into the bathroom on the opposite side of the corridor, and this time she failed to close the door by a more obvious ten inches.

I heard the click of the light switch in the bathroom, a pause, and then water running into the hand basin. There was another pause, and then the rustle of nylon against smooth flesh. Finally faint splashing sounds.

The Negro soldier was still watching the door, tempted by that open gap. He glanced behind him and then began to sidle forward. He stretched his neck to look slyly through the bathroom door, and then looked behind him again. He pulled reflectively at his lower lip, and then began to walk casually and slowly past the door, facing front but with his eyes shifting sideways.

I eased open the bedroom door. From this angle I could see the mirror over the wash basin in the bathroom. Virginia had done as I told her and removed her blouse while she washed her arms. She must have seen my reflection in the mirror too, because as I widened the gap to enter the corridor she reached both hands behind her as though to unhook the strap of her bra. The soldier had stopped dead, half-turning his back towards me, and I seized my opportunity while it was there.

I came out into the corridor fast, grabbed the guard by the shoulder, and put everything I had behind one streaking blow of my right fist. He was startled, already swinging round, and turned his jaw right into the punch. I knocked him clear out of the strap of the submachine-gun which I had caught in my left hand, and he crashed into the bathroom to go sprawling at Virginia's feet. She jumped quickly out of the way and I was already following him through with the submachine-gun levelled, but it was an unnecessary precaution. He was out cold.

Virginia looked scared and her face had gone pale again, paler than the golden skin of her midriff and shoulders. I handed her a towel to dry her arms and urged her to hurry it up, and then knelt down to check that our guard would remain asleep for a reasonable amount of time. When I straightened up again Virginia was hastily re-donning her blouse, and I paused another second to check my newly acquired firearm. It was a Stirling 9mm with one loaded magazine. The guard wasn't carrying any spares so the one magazine would have to be enough. I hooked the strap over my own shoulder and then hustled Virginia back across the corridor. Her arms were still damp and she hadn't tucked in her blouse, but now that we had taken the first step I felt a panicky urge to hurry.

The street below our window was still dark and deserted, and I quickly pulled up the blind and forced the window open. A broken leg from the two-storey drop would have been a stupid mistake, but Virginia had anticipated our need and was already stripping the top sheet from the bed. She brought it over and then hesitated, remembering the scene she had witnessed earlier. I took the sheet from her and said quietly,

"You first, Virgin. I'll lower you down."

She stared into the street, and then dragged up her courage and climbed on to the windowsill. I gave her one end of the sheet and she lowered herself full length, all the while looking down nervously over her shoulder. When she was ready I paid the sheet out slowly, leaning out as far as I dared when I came to the end so that she could safely drop the last few yards.

She twisted round immediately as her feet struck the dirt, backing up against the wall and looking anxiously in each direction. The street remained silent and deserted and that was a relief to us both. I tied my end of the sheet to the window latch, the only anchor point within reach, and by then Virginia was looking up towards me. I unslung the submachine-gun and held it up so that she could see what I intended, and then dropped it down into her hands. She caught it neatly and stepped out of the way as I scrambled through the window and followed her down the sheet. The window latch held but I didn't trust it any longer than was absolutely necessary, and seconds later I was on the ground. Virginia moved close and I retrieved the submachine-gun, taking her arm in my free hand as I swiftly checked around. We were still unobserved and I headed for the front of the hotel.

We reached the T junction with the main road, and I kept my back to the wall and very cautiously put my head around the corner. To our left was the main entrance to the hotel, with two armed sentries standing behind the protective wall of waist-high sandbags, and to our right the road led back towards the airfield. There were small groups of black soldiers visible in both directions, gossiping or wandering aimlessly in the moonless gloom, but none of them were close enough to interfere. The street lighting had either broken down or had not been switched on, and that was in our favour. Also Virginia's hearing had been very acute, and her calculation that there would be two jeeps was exactly right. One was parked directly in front of the hotel entrance, too close to the sentries and the light coming from inside, but the other was much closer, facing us and the direction in which we wanted to go.

Virginia was pressing against me in the darkness and I said softly,

"How well can you drive?"

"Fairly well."

She didn't sound very sure of herself, but there was no real choice in the matter. I whispered again,

"Then you'd better take the wheel. That'll leave me free to handle the gun. You go first and get into the driving seat. Start the engine and drive like hell. Don't stop for anything and don't even look for me. I'll cover you and jump aboard as you go past."

She nodded, for I felt the movement of her hair brash my shoulder, and then she moved out and around me, half-crouching and ready to run. I put a restraining hand on her shoulder, held her until both sentries were looking away, and then gave her a gentle push. She went like a puff of wind, fast and silent, and she was crouching down again before the bonnet of the jeep before I had the submachine-gun up to cover her. The sentries had seen nothing, and when she looked back I gave her an encouraging nod.

She circled round and climbed into the jeep, keeping the vehicle between herself and the sentries. I watched her wriggle into position behind the wheel and again I gave her a nod.

She started the engine. It roared first time and both sentries spun round to face the sound. They started to unsling their weapons but I didn't give them time. I sprang out from my corner and sprayed a sharp, warning burst from the Stirling over their heads. They dropped their guns and made a wise dive for cover as I ran out into the road. Virginia had already got the jeep in gear and moving. If she had missed the gears first time she would probably have panicked and that would have been the finish, but that first attempt was done at speed without thinking, and mercifully she got it right. She came shooting forward, going like hell and obeying my instructions so well that she almost ran me under the bonnet. I practically had to jump over it and almost missed the passing door handle on the other side. My fingers just caught to hook it open and then I hauled myself in. Virginia made another frantic gear change that would have earned any driver a winner's garland and a sportsman's kiss and we were off.

After fifty yards the main road made a sharp turn left. Virginia took it on two wheels without slowing down, screamed, braked desperately and ran slap into a barricade. I was twisted round in my seat, facing the way we had come through the back of the jeep with the Stirling ready to deter any pursuit. There was none close enough to worry about and I had started to face front as we made the turn. My feelings of relief were ripped out with Virginia's screams as I saw the two army trucks parked across the road to bar our way, and there was nothing I could do but throw up an arm to protect my face. The brakes had locked on the jeep and we skidded in a sideways swerve to crash against the front wheel of the right-side track. The jolt opened the jeep door and threw me out to land painfully and ingloriously on my backside.

For perhaps five seconds I just sat there, shocked and dazed, and then instinct had me moving again even though my brain had seized up. I was still clutching the submachine-gun in both hands and I scrambled up to run round the back of the jeep to reach the driving seat. The jeep was a crumpled wreck with water hissing out of the bonnet, and Virginia sat as though stupified behind the wheel. I heaved the door open and asked urgently,

"Virgin, are you all right?"

She didn't seem to hear, but I could see no blood and I hoped there were no broken bones. I pulled her out and mercifully she was able to stand. She moved her head and said in a distant voice,

"I think I'm all right."

This was no place to discuss it any further and I grabbed her arm and hustled her forward. There was a gap round the back of the truck and we ran through, but then we were braking to a stop almost as abruptly as the jeep had done. The road beyond was almost blocked by black soldiers and they were hurrying towards us. A chorus of yells went echoing along the street and I did a sharp about-turn and hauled Virginia back through the gap. We sprinted back to the turn in the road, swung left away from the hotel, and again the way was blocked by running soldiers.

We came to another swift halt. From our right a big Negro sprang out of shadow, bawling loudly and making a grab for Virginia. I pulled her quickly out of the way and kicked him savagely in the groin. He reeled away and there were howls all round us. The main rush came and I opened up with the Stirling over their heads. The running bodies scattered and then I caught hold of Virginia again and we turned in flight.

I had to fire another burst to clear our way past the main road turning, and then we were being chased straight back to the Impala Hotel. Howling black soldiers blocked our escape route at every other turn, and on foot we had no alternative choice. Virginia sobbed and stumbled at my side as we ran the gauntlet of clutching hands, and now I was using the submachine-gun as a club to smash my way through. The night was hideous with eager, lusting black faces, like swirling rivers flooding out from the side alleys to envelope us. Virginia fell when we were still ten yards from the hotel and I turned in the middle of the road to face the mob. There was no more hope of keeping them at bay by firing over their heads and I was ready to kill.

As I turned the rush faltered and came to a halt. I hesitated because my one submachine-gun could have been swamped by the mass of similar weapons gripped in the scores of black hands ranged against me. Then from behind my back I heard the first faint chuckles of laughter.

I turned slowly and then realised that right from the start our escape attempt had been a complete waste of time. The officers of the Revolutionary Council stood in full force outside the hotel, all of them smiling broadly. Karagwe stood in the centre of the line with Sallah beside him, and when the major-general started the first chuckle they all joined in with an uproarious show of delight.

14

New Deal

I COULD have killed them all there and then, there were enough rounds in the half-spent magazine of the Stirling, and it was a tempting thought. They were all well illuminated by the light from the hotel entrance and one clean sweep would have left the revolution leaderless. Those grinning black faces were enjoying themselves at my expense and that had me riled, but I knew better than to give way to temptation. I had to remember what would happen to Virginia and myself if there was no one left to hold back the hordes of hesitant soldiers around us, and that thought sucked all the heroics out of me. I lowered the submachine-gun and threw it away in disgust.

Karagwe stopped laughing long

enough to shout some orders and the ring of black troops lowered their own weapons and relaxed. There was no danger left in the situation, only humour, and the soldiers began to follow the example of their officers. The whole thing had become a hilarious farce. I helped Virginia to her feet and with peals of laughter following us we stumbled over to the hotel. Karagwe and Sallah parted to let us through, and the major-general slapped me cheerfully on the back.

"An excellent try, Major M'Call. Excellent! We expected that you would attempt something of this nature."

He followed us into the hotel foyer with most of his brother officers. Only one of the lieutenant-colonels stayed outside to disperse the troops. Virginia was badly shaken and I had to stop and give her time to steady herself. Outside the roars of laughter continued, but Karagwe tapped me on the shoulder and when I turned I saw that his mirth had started to recede. He said seriously,

"However, Major M'Call, I trust that you now realise that any kind of escape is impossible. Your only hope of leaving Kaduna lies in complete cooperation with me."

I nodded wearily, the lesson had been rammed home and I had learned it well. I could only hope that Virginia had learned it too.

★ ★ ★

We were taken back to the same room, and Sallah made a pointed joke of asking whether we would require any more sheets for the bed. We had to listen to more laughter as he left, and as he went through the door he absent-mindedly remarked that there would now be two sentries in the corridor instead of one. He closed the door and I could hear him chuckling as he went away.

I waited a moment, and then I turned to Virginia. I hadn't yet been able to find out whether she had suffered any serious hurt, and I asked her gently.

She shook her head vaguely.

"No, Mike, I don't think so. I'm just shaken. I banged my knee when the jeep crashed but that's all. Everything is hazy, it happened so fast. It hasn't really sunk in yet."

She sat down on the edge of the bed and I sat beside her. There didn't seem to be anything else to do. She was trembling and after a moment she turned and put her arms around me, leaning her face against my shoulder. She was quiet and I remembered what she had once said, that her father had been a major in the Royal Marines. I wondered how her father would have comforted her now, and carefully I began to stroke her hair. She was so very young and defeated, but she hadn't cracked as I had feared she might. She had a different brand of courage to mine, and lots more of it. After a while she stopped trembling, and then more long minutes passed before she stirred and asked,

"What are we going to do now, Mike?"

I said quietly, "I shall have to co-operate with Karagwe, as he said, there's no alternative. It's the only way in which I can hope to get you out of here and back to Lagos. And remember that it is important that you get back. Your knowledge is important."

She nodded her head slowly, and I was relieved that for once I had phrased my words just right. Our escape attempt had at least served one small purpose, for she was more willing to trust me now that I had been prepared to make it. We talked some more but her spirits were dulled again, and finally I made her lay back on the bed. I covered her with a sheet, and then switched off the light and went to sit in the chair by the window. After an hour I knew she was asleep, but I remained awake and thinking. I spent most of that night in thinking.

★ ★ ★

An hour after dawn one of our guards brought us breakfast; a jug of sour coffee, some stale bread rolls, and a small amount of butter and jam. It wasn't much but I persuaded Virginia to eat most of her share. When the guard returned he brought a fresh jug of iced water and for the rest of the morning we just sat around. The room filled with heat but there were no interruptions. We might have been forgotten.

The atmosphere made me sweat, and I took off my shirt rather than soil it. Virginia hesitated longer, but eventually she went out to the bathroom and came back with a large towel wrapped around her and her blouse and skirt washed out in her hand. She hung the damp clothes over a chair to dry, and then sat down on the bed again in her panties and bra. She was much more trusting today, but she kept the big towel close in case anyone else walked in. To occupy her mind I got her to talk about the village school where she had worked for eighteen months as a volunteer teacher. It was too hot for talk but she talked anyway, drawing some sad pleasure from her memories. My life story was longer but less presentable so I kept it quiet.

It was past noon when Sallah came to fetch me for another interview. Virginia covered herself quickly with the towel when he knocked and then I moved to open the door. He was in uniform again, polite and smiling as always, and after brief courtesies he led me back down to the conference room.

The captain and one of the majors were missing, but the rest of the Revolutionary Council were ranged as before behind the large table, with Karagwe occupying the central position. Sallah and I sat facing them on the same two chairs as yesterday and formal greetings were made. Nobody mentioned my discomfiture of last night, and the general atmosphere suggested that as long as I was prepared to behave myself in the future they were prepared to forgive and forget. They had enjoyed their hearty laugh, but now it was time to renew the serious discussion of business. Karagwe was shuffling three flimsy scraps of paper in his hands, and his bearded face wore a grim expression. He said bluntly,

"Major M'Call, we have now received the answers to those three cables you despatched from Lagos. They were delivered to the Ambassadors Hotel early this morning, and a friend of ours was able to bribe a desk clerk into revealing their contents. Would you care to hear the results?"

My mouth felt dry but I nodded in assent. Karagwe glanced through the printed slips in his hand and read out:

"From Bordeaux, a Monsieur Paul Chabrand; a one-word answer — *negative*.

"From Marseilles, a Monsieur Andre Renard; a one-word answer — *negative*.

"And from Genoa, Senore Giuseppe Tambroni; a final one-word answer. It is again *negative.*"

He dropped the scraps of paper carelessly on to the table, and then regarded me with ominous eyes.

"I take it that these answers mean that your friends have nothing to offer. They have no movable supplies that are not subject to normal clearance papers?"

My backbone felt as though it had started to crumble and subside down into my belly, but I had to admit that he had read the cables perfectly correctly. Karagwe picked them up again, crushed them in his fist and then tossed them over his shoulder. It was a symbolic prelude to his next sentence.

"In that case, Major M'Call, I can only hope that you have followed my advice, and thought of some other means of solving our mutual problem."

I had, but it could land me in a worse mess than I was in now and I preferred to stall. I said hopefully,

"I can try some more contacts in the United States. They operate on a larger and more reliable scale than the European dealers, but of course the shipping arrangements could take longer. If you give me time I'm sure I can fix something."

"We have no time!" Karagwe clenched his hands together in one big, threatening fist as he spoke. "As soon as those armoured cars and rifles come ashore in Lagos General Daniel Makefa will be re-equipping his troops and sending them here against us. You must offer me something definite."

"There's an American dealer who might — "

"Might is not definite, Major M'Call."

"Then I can't damned well help you!"

I snapped it back at him and for a moment we glared at each other across the table. Then he said tartly,

"If you really cannot help us that is a pity. It means that you will no longer have any claim, or right to expect our protection. Neither you nor the girl."

"And what does that mean?"

Karagwe smiled. "It means that you will both be asked to leave this hotel. We shall have no more desire to entertain you as our guests. What happens to you in the street is your own affair."

I stared at him, remembering the previous night, and the unknown blonde wife of the unknown factory manager. His face offered me no hope, showing only triumph with his winning card. His fellow officers were like puppet images of himself, lacking only the bristly beard, and when I looked at Sallah sitting next to me his face was bland and expressionless,

I said helplessly, "But what am I supposed to do?"

Karagwe said bluntly, "You are an arms dealer, Major. That is your business. I am sure that if you are willing you are best fitted to answer your own question."

There was silence, and I could only see one way out, the result of all that heavy thinking that had kept me awake throughout the night. I said reluctantly,

"All right, but first let me repeat myself for the last time. I can't provide you with an arms contract with Trans-Global. I can't stop Trans-Global's contract with Makefa from going through. And without a long time delay I can't provide you with a private deal. There's only one possible thing that I can try to help you, and I can't guarantee that that will succeed."

"And what is that one possible thing?"

I drew a deep breath and then explained.

"I can try and work a switch so that you can obtain those arms that are already being delivered to Makefa. There's nothing I can do about the armoured cars, he'll have to keep those, but I might be able to get you the rifles."

Karagwe looked doubtful but interested, he conferred with the rest of the table, all of them suddenly talking rapidly in Hausa, and then he turned suspicious eyes back to me.

"Explain how this may be possible?"

I had to convince him now, and that wasn't going to be easy because I hadn't yet convinced myself. However, I tried.

"As you know the arms shipment for Makefa will arrive in Lagos aboard the *African Rose*, she's due in Lagos either tomorrow afternoon or tomorrow night. Now, I'm expected to be there at the unloading. Makefa will want to check the shipment when it arrives, and it's part of my job to be there and make sure that he's satisfied. That means that I shall know exactly where and in which warehouse the arms will be stored before being moved out to the army camp.

"The second point is that Trans-Global prefers to send their arms shipments under another name, to avoid any undue curiosity *en route*. In this instance the cases are marked farm implements, and only the ship's officers and the necessary port officials are supposed to know what the cases really contain. As an extra precaution a genuine consignment of farm implements is also included in the ship's cargo. The cases are all identical, but the ones containing the arms are marked with a special cross. That's the only way to read the difference, and a small group of men working hard through the night should be able to swap over the bulk of the cases. The arms will be moved out in unguarded trucks which can be easily ambushed, and Makefa's troops will be left guarding the farm tools." I smiled forcibly and finished. "Makefa's soldiers won't be very dangerous if they have to be re-equipped with spades and pickaxes."

Karagwe wrinkled his brows and demanded.

"How will you get into the warehouse,

and how can you hope to work undisturbed?"

That problem had worried me too, but I said hopefully,

"I won't know that until I know the precise location and layout of the warehouse. I'll have to work out the details on the spot."

"Daniel Makefa is no child, he will have the sense to post guards."

"Then I'll have to avoid them. They won't expect anything like this, and because of that it should be possible."

Karagwe tugged at his beard, staring into my face. He didn't trust me and he didn't believe it was possible, and yet at the same time the very idea of stealing Makefa's arms shipment had a definite appeal. He consulted his council of officers, all of whom seemed equally undecided, and after a storm of unintelligible jabber in Hausa he returned to English and to me. We argued and bargained for a long, sweating, frustrating hour, and finally he accepted that I had nothing else to offer, and that it was mostly my neck that I would be risking anyway.

He said at last,

"Very well, Major M'Call, I agree. You will be taken back to Lagos and given the opportunity to make this crazy idea work. But the girl will remain here in Kaduna — as a gesture of your good faith, you understand?"

I understood, I had expected it, and I pitched into the next stage of the argument.

"I can't allow that General. And I think you know why. You and your officer's don't have sufficient control over your own troops. I saw what happened to that white woman in the street yesterday. She was dead before your soldiers could be pulled away. Major Sallah said that she ran away because she was frightened, and Miss West is also a highly nervous young woman. If I left her alone she might make the same foolish mistake, and I won't risk that!"

My response opened another thirty

minutes of verbal war and heated words. Tempers slipped and Karagwe beat his fist upon the table but I stuck bitterly to my guns. If Virginia was to be held in Kaduna then I stayed with her, it was as simple as that. Finally the lieutenant-colonel on Karagwe's right, the only man who seemed to have any influence, made a suggestion that the major-general was able to accept. He listened, and then translated into English for me.

"We will offer a compromise, Major M'Call. The girl will be returned to Lagos, but she will be accompanied by Major Sallah and will remain in his custody until you have completed your task. This way we shall still have our hostage for your good behaviour, and yet you will have no need to fear that the girl may be assaulted by some of our more unruly soldiers here in Kaduna. I think that this arrangement must be satisfactory to both sides."

I could have blessed the lieutenant-colonel, for it was exactly the arrangement I had hoped for but had not dared to suggest. I had never expected that they would release us both, but in Lagos there was always hope that I could work a fast move over Major Sallah. There was more chance there than in Kaduna anyway. I argued less strongly for another ten minutes just to maintain the appearance of reluctance, and then I capitulated and went back to discussing the details.

15

Fast Talk

IT was the same Beagle B.206
that took us back to Lagos, again
making the flight during the hours
of darkness and landing an hour before
dawn. We touched down on a flat strip
of beach with the sea rolling in from
one side, and a dark jungle of flowering
palm fronds on the other. The Beagle
floundered and skidded before it came
to a standstill, and I had the feeling
that the pilot enjoyed its antics even
less than I did. A beach wasn't the ideal
landing place, but I guessed that he also
had no real choice in these matters.

We had the same escort as before,
Sallah now out of uniform and back
in his dark blue suit, and the three
Negro sergeants all in civilian clothes.
We descended from the plane and were

hustled quickly out of the way under the shadow of the palm trees. The twin engines never stopped turning and as soon as we were clear they gathered power again and the Beagle taxied forward into take-off. It wheeled back over the jungle and disappeared inland, and the whole operation had taken only a matter of minutes.

Sallah gave orders and we were marched along the beach. Virginia kept very close to me and accepted my guiding hand on her arm. She was mostly silent and it seemed that events had moved too fast for her. Also her thoughts and feelings had now turned full circle and she had found some flimsy cause to trust in me. Perhaps she didn't really expect that I could do anything worth while, but there was nothing and no one else on which she could pin any hopes. I had explained my new deal with Karagwe and she had considered that a kind of moral betrayal, and yet she accepted that there was nothing else that I could have done.

After half a mile we turned away from the beach through the palm trees and emerged on to a tarmac road. There was a Land-Rover waiting with a driver, and after cautiously establishing identities we went forward. One of the sergeants joined the driver in the front, but the rest of us climbed into the back. There was no waste of time, for Sallah was in a hurry, and almost immediately we were speeding along the last twenty-mile lap into Lagos.

Dawn was filtering through the swiftly passing trees in long flashes of broken light, waking the birds and turning the blacker patches of shadow into green. The Land-Rover swayed and jolted and left a continuous swirl of dust in its tracks. The lighter shadows were an ever-changing pattern and the miles rushed by. A signpost went past that read five miles into Lagos, and Sallah casually rapped out an order. The driver glanced back, hesitated, and then put his foot on the brake and stopped. Sallah looked at me and said calmly,

"This is where we say a temporary good-bye, Major M'Call. From here you can walk into the city."

I stared at him.

"That doesn't make sense, why leave me here?"

"But it does make sense. I am not naïve enough to let you learn where I intend to hold Miss West, and therefore it is best that we part before entering Lagos. You will return to the Ambassadors Hotel, and I will contact you there after the *African Rose* has docked and unloaded her cargo. Then we will be able to discuss the final details of our plans."

I should have expected something of the sort but I hadn't. Sallah smiled calmly and waited, and one of the sergeants began to idly scratch his own chest, his fingers very close to the shoulder holster fitted under his left arm. I looked at Virginia but she could only shrug helplessly. There was nothing that I could do except get out and drop down into the road.

Sallah followed me for a final word. He said shrewdly,

"If you are successful in obtaining those arms for us, Major, then the Revolutionary Council has agreed that you will be paid the sum of ten thousand stirling pounds. We feel that if there is a definite reward then you will be inclined to put more endeavour into your efforts. And of course, Miss West will be returned to you."

"Thanks very much, but I never did guarantee success. I'll do my best, but what happens if I fail?"

"Then there will be no reward."

"And the girl?"

"My orders are to take her back to Kaduna. There she will probably be released."

I knew what he meant, released into a street full of uncontrolled black soldiers. He was smiling at me almost sympathetically and I said slowly,

"We understand each other, Major Sallah, and — "

" — And one day you are going to kill me?"

It was not what I had meant to say, but it was near enough. Sallah smiled as though he had won another victory and then wished me good-bye and good luck. He returned to the Land-Rover and it drove off towards Lagos, leaving me coughing in its swirl of dust.

My curses were more than violent, even for an ex-sergeant in the marines, but after I had spat them and the dust out of my system I began the long sweating walk.

★ ★ ★

I walked three miles before I was able to wave down a ramshackle bus that carried me the rest of the way. The wooden seats were weighed down with colourful black mammies, an army of cheeky black children, vast baskets of

271

vegetable produce and a few black husbands. Everybody got out at the final stop which was an open air street market, and I managed to push my way out of the babbling chaos to find a taxi that returned me to the Ambassadors Hotel.

The mermaid fountain in the foyer was still making tinkling water music as though I had never been away, and I brushed aside the enquiring remarks at the reception desk as I collected my key. I went direct to the lift and up to my room. There was one thing I needed more than anything else and I stripped off my grubby clothes and spent ten minutes of cold luxury under the shower. There had been a shower in the bathroom of the Impala Hotel in Kaduna, but there it had been out of order. When I had revived my wilted frame I found some clean clothes, and then I hunted out the bottle of Seagrams and mixed myself a healthy drink. It was early, but I hadn't had one for almost two days, and I needed some help to figure out my next move. I hadn't calculated on not knowing where Virginia would be held prisoner, and that was a damned great spanner chucked right through the middle of all my fragile plans.

I knew that I wouldn't have long before I could expect visitors, but the first knock sounded before I was half-way through my drink. I swore because I had hoped for a little more peace than that, but the knock came again and I had to go to the door. I was startled to find Kamau standing there, looking as fit as ever and without even a scuff or a tear in his lieutenant's uniform. My surprise must have showed for he smiled broadly.

"Welcome, Major M'Call. The reception desk informed me the moment that you returned. It is a pleasure to have you back."

I said slowly, "It's a pleasure to see you again. I was convinced that you were dead."

He shook his head, still smiling.

"No, Major, your kidnappers were very poor shots. I still have bandages around my arm but nothing worse. They spoiled one uniform jacket and knocked me off my feet but that was all. I am only sorry that I was too slow and clumsy to stop them."

I said wryly, "Don't worry about it. I didn't do so well myself."

Kamau nodded, but then became serious.

"I shall be interested to know what has happened to you, Major, but General Makefa has also been advised of your return and he too is impatient to hear your story. My orders are to take you to him immediately, so perhaps we can talk in the car."

He didn't leave me much room to argue so I finished my drink and we went. He was driving the same Jaguar staff car and on the way I went through a quick dress rehearsal of the explanations I meant to give Makefa. Kamau listened and asked a few polite questions without displaying any outward doubts, and I could only hope that Makefa would be equally convinced.

When we arrived at Army Head-quarters I was kept waiting for thirty minutes in an outer office because the General was in conference. It was the first time that I had not been ushered straight through, and a significant way of telling me that I had lost some of my former V.I.P. status. Noticeably no one emerged from the inner sanctum when I was at last allowed to go in. Makefa sat back behind his ship-of-state desk with his arms folded across his chest, his bearing somewhere between that of a lonely monarch and a waiting judge. He smiled when I reached the desk, but the smile and his polite tone were both too exaggerated to hold any reassurance.

"Major M'Call, it is good of you to return to us. I had begun to fear that your abrupt disappearance would be permanent."

I smiled too, and hoped that mine

wasn't such an obvious fake.

"I had very similar fears, General, I can assure you. I'm both surprised and relieved to be back in Lagos."

"Perhaps you will be good enough to tell me what has happened?"

I nodded and sat down. I hadn't been invited to sit, but I was pretending hard that I had no worries and that I hadn't noticed the lack of invitation. I said frankly,

"It's a long story, General. I was kidnapped by a group of your rivals and taken north to Kaduna." I gave him the full details, except that I didn't mention Virginia West, and it was not until I reached my dealings with the Revolutionary Council that I began to alter the facts. I didn't dare gamble that he didn't know about those cables from Europe, and so I had to build my story very gingerly indeed from a selection of half-truths. Makefa's expression was unreadable now, but I tried to radiate honesty as I talked.

"The rebels wanted to buy arms, that

was the purpose of the kidnapping, but I was able to convince them that there was no possibility that they might be supplied by Trans-Global. When they accepted that they insisted that I put them in touch with a private dealer, and I was forced to send cables to three of my contacts in the arms trade in Europe. Fortunately the replies were all negative. After that I promised to find them a private dealer in America, but I persuaded them that I could work best here in Lagos where there are more facilities for communication. They were reluctant to release me, but last night they flew me back to a beach west of Lagos and turned me loose." I paused and then added, "Naturally I do not consider myself bound by any promises that were extracted under pressure. I have no intentions for helping Major-General Karagwe to obtain a supply of arms."

There was a long silence. Makefa simply stared at me across the wide desk and the effect was better than the glare of a dozen arc-lamps. I found myself blinking, and then felt a faint rush of sweat bubbles forming over my eyes. Then Makefa said,

"I find it hard to believe that Major-General Karagwe released you so easily. I know the man and it does not fit his character. Surely there was some incentive for you to keep your promises?"

I nodded. "There was ten thousand pounds worth of incentive. But they could double-cross me as easily as I'm double-crossing them, and I'm not fool enough to stick my neck out. I already make a better than average commission from legal transactions. I don't need to go crooked."

Makefa nodded slowly and then asked,

"And what about the girl?"

It was obvious that Kamau would have mentioned Virginia, but I kept a blank face.

"I don't understand."

"The girl from the Corsair motor

car. The girl who was kidnapped with you."

"But she was killed in the crash. Lieutenant Kamau was on the scene within seconds, surely he told you that?"

Makefa shook his head. "Lieutenant Kamau saw the girl taken with you in the kidnappers' car."

I stared at him, as though this was news. Then I said bitterly,

"I was drugged. I didn't know. They told me she was killed in the car crash and I believed them. If Kamau saw her alive then they must have murdered her later and hidden her body before we boarded the plane. It's the only answer."

It was the only answer that I could invent to cover Virginia's disappearance, for I had to prevent him from guessing that she was still being held hostage for my good behaviour. If I could convince him that she was dead, and if he wasn't aware that those cables to Europe had been despatched before I was taken north to Kaduna, then I could talk and bluff my way out of the interview. If not I was in deep trouble.

Makefa brooded thoughtfully, and then asked,

"Who was the girl?"

I told him. It was a fair bet that he had traced the crashed Corsair back to the car hire firm and already knew her name, so I had to stay close to the truth. I told him all the facts that he would know, and a few that he probably didn't, pretending only that I didn't know why she wanted to visit the British High Commission at that late hour.

"I knew that she was wanted by the Lagos Police," I admitted. "I had a visit from a Captain Shabani earlier in that day. The girl came back later and asked me to accompany her to the High Commission. She wouldn't explain what was wrong, but she was very frightened and seemed to think that the police would try to stop her. I couldn't persuade her to go to Shabani, so finally I agreed to do as she asked. I knew that the High Commissioner would inform the police anyway if any crime had been committed." I paused and then concluded, "Now that she's dead we won't know what trouble she was in, unless you can find out from Captain Shabani."

That was dangerous ground, but I had to calculate that there was most probably contact between them already. Makefa frowned for a moment, and then switched back to the subject of my dealings with the Revolutionary Council. He demanded names and details of all the officers I had seen, and I answered as frankly as possible, although I could only name Karagwe and Sallah. Mercifully the ranks and descriptions I could offer helped him to identify the others and proved that I was trying to be helpful. There were a million other questions about conditions in Kaduna, the location of the rebel HQ, troop deployment and morale, and I answered them all as accurately as I could. He fired them endlessly until my brain reeled, and when he had exhausted my knowledge he went back to a savage re-examination of my personal story and motives. I spent two hours of fast, solid talking, and at the end of it Makefa still reserved his doubts. However, he had failed to trap me or trick me with his questions and at last he grew tired.

He said grimly, "Very well, Major M'Call, I will accept your story. But I shall expect you to inform me immediately when the rebels attempt to contact you again. In the meantime Lieutenant Kamau will be reassigned to your protection, and you will be well advised not to elude him in the future."

I knew what he meant, but I had to bottle up the helpless frustration inside me. I was free, but only on parole, and it would be impossible to track down Sallah with Kamau sticking like a leech to my heels.

16

Arms Ship

AT ten-thirty that night the *African Rose* arrived in Lagos Harbour. She dropped anchor for the night, and then at seven o'clock the next morning she was brought into a vacant berth against the quayside. The cargo hatches were opened and she began unloading three hours later, and by then I was present in the blaring sunshine to check the crates ashore. I felt rough and bleary-eyed after a night of sleepless worrying over Virginia, but I hadn't a clue where she might be held prisoner, and I couldn't risk dodging Kamau until I had a definite lead. I could only wait for Sallah to contact me and hope that luck would start to break in my direction from there. If it didn't then my headache was going to be doubled.

The ship was a fourteen thousand ton freighter, flying the red duster and the white flag with the red rose emblem of the Rose Line Shipping Company. By freighter standards she was quite presentable, and the only rust mark on her hull was the brown smear below the hoisted anchor. Kamau stood beside me on the quay and we watched the Negro stevedores swarm over the ship, and beside us stood a Major Bumendu who was Makefa's official representative. The major was also in command of the platoon of armed Federal troops who ringed this particular corner of the dockyard.

The winches rattled and screamed, and one by one the armoured cars were swung ashore. They were fifty Mark Two Ferret scout cars, fast-moving, hard-hitting, and the ideal spearhead for infantry units operating over rough country. They were lowered gently, unshackled, and pushed to one side. Then in convoys of ten they were driven off direct to the army camp by two-man crews from the waiting troops, followed by the heavy truck that was to bring them back to pick up the next batch. The atmosphere was a confusion of dust, heat glare, and the sounds of raucous voices, clanking machinery and the revving of engines, but the two officers beside me were unruffled by it all. Kamau quietly admired each new scout car as it was swung into view, no doubt dreaming of the charge he was hoping to lead into Kaduna, while Bumendu carefully checked the serial numbers of each vehicle against the clipboard he held in his hand.

When the cars were cleared away the crates containing the rifles began to emerge from the forward hold. Ten thousand Belgian F.A.L. rifles, each fitted with a twenty-round magazine, packed in crates of fifty equalling two hundred crates all told: plus a further two hundred identical crates containing farm implements shipped by Alfred Cross & Sons of Bedford,

England, the name and description that was stamped in big black letters on all four hundred crates. They were shifted into the adjoining unloading shed, and there Bumendu and I supervised their separation. The job lasted us all afternoon, and although we had moved in from the direct heat on the quayside my shirt was again ruined by sweat and dust.

The farm tools came ashore first and were stacked to one side, and then a separate block was made with the last two hundred crates, each distinguished by a two inch high X stamped neatly in one corner. When they were all ashore the heavy steel shutters that formed the doors of the loading shed were lowered and locked, and the remaining cargo that the *African Rose* had to leave in Lagos was either taken directly away or stored in one of the other sheds further along the quayside.

We had to wait for Makefa to arrive and check the shipment, suffering in the stuffy gloom of the long warehouse, and I casually fished for information from Bumendu. I learned that the rifles would remain under guard throughout the night, and would then be moved out to the army camp the following morning. Later in the day the genuine cases of farm implements would be shifted to another warehouse outside the docks. That was all I wanted to know, and I had already noted that there were some useful sky lights fitted along the roof. I hoped that I wouldn't have to use either item of information, but for the moment I had to try and cover all the possible bets.

Makefa finally arrived in full uniform, accompanied by two other staff officers, and looking more than unusually jovial. Kamau was standing by with a crowbar and promptly opened up one of the marked crates. Makefa lifted out one of the rifles, handling it with expert care, beaming and expressing his satisfaction. Kamau drew out two more of the brand new weapons and offered them to the two staff officers who made pretty much the same response. When the admiration ceremony was over Kamau returned the rifles to the case and nailed down the lid. However, Makefa wasn't allowing his pleasure to affect his doubting nature, and three more crates had to be broken open at random before he was convinced that everything was in order. He conferred with Bumendu and checked the calculations on the major's clipboard, and then turned to me.

"Everything seems to be as it should be, Major M'Call. I have already inspected the armoured cars that have been brought out to the army camp, and they too are exactly what are needed to our requirements. All that remains is the matter of payment, and if you care to follow me back to Army HQ that can be settled without delay."

"That's fine," I said. "I never refuse to discuss money."

Makefa smiled as though we had always been the best of friends, and then began to move out of the warehouse. He was already discussing the broad details of his planned moves against Karagwe with his companions, but when we emerged into the sunlight he paused to make sure that Bumendu understood his orders for the night.

Bumendu nodded. "Yes, General — a permanent guard outside the warehouse, and at all the dock gates, and regular patrols throughout the dockyard. Nobody is to be allowed to approach without your personal authorisation."

Makefa expressed his approval, and then turned to climb into his waiting staff car. It was another black Jaguar saloon, and when it moved off Kamau and I got into our own car and followed. The winches were still working aboard the *African Rose* as we drove away from the quayside, swinging boxes and bales endlessly out of the hold, but I wasn't sorry to be leaving all the activity behind. All I wanted to see was a cheque and a drink, and then time to start thinking again about my own problems.

★ ★ ★

When we were alone in his office Makefa sat down at his desk and using a gold-capped fountain pen he carelessly scribbled out the cheque. He tore the pink slip out of the book, blotted it, and passed it over the desk. It was made out to Trans-Global Arms, to be cashed in the city of London, and the total figure was two hundred and forty thousand pounds. My five per cent commission out of that would make a respectable twelve thousand, and this time I felt that I had really earned it. Makefa had signed below the name of the Finance Minister for the Nigerian Government, making a heavier and more positive scrawl, and I smiled at it almost fondly.

Makefa smiled too and then offered me the fountain pen and a receipt. I made my autograph too, and then handed them back. Makefa pushed them to one side after only a casual glance and then brought out the whisky bottle and two glasses.

"Another celebration I think, Major." His face was still wreathed in smiles. "And this time we shall have doubles."

I nodded agreement. He poured the two glasses, squirted a splash of soda into each, and then I made a diplomatic toast.

"To your success, General. You now have all that you need to march your troops north. Let us drink to a speedy end to the rebellion, and a fast return for unity to Nigeria."

"Thank you, Major M'Call, and we will also drink to your safe and speedy return to London."

We both honoured the toast, and then I remarked tentatively,

"I assume that you have no problems with ammunition?"

He shook his head. "None at all. We have adequate stocks and regular sources of supply. I am afraid that for the moment we can do no further business."

"But perhaps in the future," I

suggested. "I can assure you that the delays you have experienced over this transaction are not normal. They were the result of possibly unique circumstances. Deliveries from Trans-Global are generally much more prompt."

Makefa dismissed the subject with a movement of his hand and said pleasantly,

"I fully understand. And perhaps in the future there will be the opportunity for us to do business again." He paused and then added, "In the meantime I should like you to accept a small personal gift."

He opened his desk drawer and took out a small narrow booklet, passing it over almost apologetically. It was a B.O.A.C. airline ticket, and when I opened it up I saw that I had been reserved a first class seat on a London bound plane departing at noon the following day, leaving me less than seventeen hours in Lagos. I looked up slowly and Makefa was still smiling.

"That is the next available plane, Major. It occurred to me that the rebels may try to exert some more pressure upon you to arrange a deal for them, and so for your own safety I think that it is best that you depart from Nigeria as soon as possible."

17

Night Folly

KAMAU drove me back to the Ambassadors and when I told him that I wouldn't be going out during the evening he nodded sociably but departed no further than the lounge. I took the lift up to the third floor and then came back quietly down the stairs. As I suspected Kamau had now moved a chair out into the foyer so that he could watch all the exits. I swore and then went up to my room. There would be a staff exit at the back, but I had a horrible feeling that that would be guarded too.

I showered and dressed and then rang down room service to send me up a large plate of sandwiches and a bottle of cold lager. The sandwiches contained chicken again but I ate without appetite.

Sallah had given me no clue as to how he would try to contact me and I could do nothing but sit around and wait for him to make the first move. I wasn't sure how he would be able to reach me inside the hotel, but if I went out then I might miss him altogether. I stayed close to the phone, wondering if he would try to make some kind of guarded call and hoping that he wouldn't. It was almost certain that the reception desk would have been instructed to let Kamau listen in to any calls to my room.

When the sandwich plate was collected I asked for a new bottle of Seagram's V.O. to be sent up, but when it came I drank sparingly. Tonight I couldn't afford to get drunk. My vital seventeen hours began to shrink slowly but inexorably with the contents of the bottle, and it seemed that all that I was pouring down my throat was frustration. Sallah wouldn't know that I had a time limit in which to get out of Lagos, but surely he must realise that any action over the arms would have to be taken tonight before they could be moved. I watched the clock and cursed him repeatedly.

By eleven o'clock I was badly worried, and convinced that I should have left the hotel where it would have been easier for him to make contact. I hesitated over whether it would be too late to go out now, but if I went out openly then Kamau would insist that he accompanied me, and if I made a furtive exit to avoid Kamau then I could easily miss Sallah as well. It was a ticklish problem with no sure answer, and I couldn't make a decision.

Midnight came, and I was a third of the way through the Seagram's. I called a halt and screwed the cap on firmly, and then put the bottle out of sight. I took another cold shower to sober and freshen myself up, and I didn't hear Sallah enter the outer room. When I came out again he was sitting in my vacated chair, smiling and holding a revolver casually against his right leg.

He knew damned well that I meant to double-cross him if I got the chance.

However, I was relieved to see him. I said grimly,

"You took your time, but how did you get in?"

He shrugged carelessly. "I came in through the kitchens, and had to wait until all the staff had finished working. Makefa has posted watchdogs back and front, by the way, but I was guided by a kitchen porter who is a relative of one of my sergeants. It was quite simple."

"And why the hardware?"

He raised the revolver an inch, shrugged again and then let it fall back against his leg.

"Just a precaution, Major. It seemed possible that you might have worked with General Makefa to plan a trap for me, and I am rather cowardly where my personal safety is concerned. I would not hesitate to kill you if I thought that it was threatened." He smiled sadly and added, "My colleagues also have permission to enjoy, and then kill the girl if I do not return within a specified time."

I said bleakly, "That's not very friendly."

"Perhaps not, but I trust that you still intend to cooperate in the matter of switching those cases of arms?"

I nodded. Until I could grab that gun and beat a few necessary facts out of him there was no other way.

"It can be done. The arms are stored in number three unloading shed, with a strong guard posted outside, but I think we can by-pass the guards from the roof of shed number two. There was a stack of twenty-foot timbers waiting to be loaded further along the quayside, and one of them should just bridge the gap between the two sheds. We're going to need a thirty-foot rope, a torch, a tin of black paint, a small paintbrush, and a carpenter's plane; plus three or four strong men who can work silently and are fool enough to risk their necks."

"They can all be provided."

"Good, and it must be done tonight. Both the arms, and the identical crates of farm tools are due to be moved tomorrow. The farm tools are being taken to a larger warehouse outside the docks. I don't know exactly where. You'll have to find that out. Once you have that information you can hi-jack the trucks when they arrive at the warehouse and you'll have the arms."

Sallah smiled. "I have already done all the necessary research, and everything is arranged for tomorrow. All that remains is for the cases to be exchanged tonight."

He stood up and added, "And now it is time we started to move. The night is short and it is dangerous for us to discuss details here. You will precede me, Major, and I will guide you out by my route of entry."

I couldn't argue with the gun so I picked up my jacket and did as he suggested.

We encountered no one as we descended through the staff area, and

I got no chance to try any story-book heroics. Sallah gave his directions softly and stayed cautiously behind me. The route led down a flight of back stairs, and then through a maze of sculleries, gleaming sinks, stoves and hanging pots and pans. We emerged through a side door into an enclosed yard that smelt of ripe garbage, and then had to climb over a locked gate to get into a side street.

I climbed first, and there was a glimmer of hope inside me that Sallah might leave himself vulnerable to attack as he followed. If I could get that gun away from him and force him to tell me where Virginia was being held then I would gamble that I could reach her before she was killed. But then I pulled myself over the gate and found one of Sallah's sergeants waiting to greet me on the other side. He too had a revolver and I knew that they were giving me no chances at all.

With a double escort I was hurriedly marched away, and after five minutes we reached the Land-Rover that was parked in darkness up another side street. As we approached I saw that the black Jaguar with the dented flank was just in front of it, and that inside the Land-Rover the other two sergeants were patiently waiting. Sallah had obviously thought ahead for all three of his subordinates were dressed in soiled pants and sweat shirts, which made them identical to the hordes of stevedores who had been thronging around the *African Rose* earlier in the day. When we were all in the Land-Rover Sallah gave some swift orders and one of the men slipped out and hurried away. Then the major turned to me.

"We have a coil of rope, but the other items I did not anticipate. However, they can be found, and while we wait you can tell me exactly what you intend to do."

I told him how I had planned it, and he listened without interruption. At the finish it was one of the sergeants who asked the only question, a query about the strength of Bumendu's patrols, and I realised that they all spoke English. I had to admit that the whole operation would be very chancey and hoped that they would be deterred. Unfortunately their discipline was far above average for African troops, and they were prepared to accept the risks. Sallah didn't allow me to elaborate on all the many things that could go wrong, but broke in to give me my final instructions.

"When the job is done you had best return to the Ambassadors Hotel. Now that you know the way you should be able to get back without being seen, and although Makefa may suspect you be will not be able to prove that you had any part in tonight's work. I shall have to hold the girl until we actually have the arms, to guard against any last minute betrayal, you understand, but as soon as it is possible she will be released."

"And what guarantee do I have?"

"You have my word as an officer, Major."

I didn't much care for it, but I had no choice, and then he startled me by saying,

"Sergeant Sakara will be the senior man in my absence, Major M'Call, but they will all be under your orders. I wish you every success."

He started to get out of the Land-Rover and I grabbed his arm.

"Wait a minute. I thought you were coming too."

He half-turned, firmly removed my hand, and smiled.

"No, Major. It would be too easy for you to give the alarm and hand all four of us over to Bumendu's troops. My men are reliable and you should be able to manage without me. I prefer to stay well back, and provide insurance for my men by watching personally over the girl."

Sakara was the biggest of the sergeants, the one who had waited for us outside the hotel yard, and he smiled too and pointed his revolver idly at my left ear. Sallah got down into the road and I knew that my last hopes of a double-cross were leaving with him. There was nothing left but to go through with switching the arms as I had described. I was cursing inwardly but I had another question before he vanished.

"What about my ten thousand pounds?"

He paused, and this time his smile showed a flicker of admiration.

"A sensible question, Major. A signed cheque on a Swiss bank will be made out to you and given to the girl. She can bring it to you when she is released. Again you have my word as an officer."

Again it wasn't much of a guarantee, but if I had to stick my neck out I saw no reason why I shouldn't at least try to salvage anything that was possible out of the mess. I nodded, and watched him get into the Jaguar and drive away into the night. I was powerless to do anything else.

An hour later Sakara was easing the Land-Rover into a dockside alley. The third sergeant had returned ten minutes previously with all the equipment I had requested stuffed into a knapsack, and we had got under way immediately. I didn't ask where he had procured the necessary items at this hour of night, but merely assumed that he had close contacts or friends. When the Land-Rover stopped Sakara switched off the engine and lights and for a few moments we waited in darkness. There was no challenge, and finally we got down into the alley.

Sakara smiled and said, "There are so many military vehicles in Lagos that I do not think ours will attract any undue attention. Even so we must hurry."

I hoped that he was right and I agreed that we should hurry, especially as the alley reeked of refuse and urine. The two junior sergeants shouldered the knapsack and the coil of rope, and with Sakara leading we moved fast in short running bursts through a black maze of more alleyways, stopping at every corner, and finally coming out on to a road. On the opposite side of the broken road surface was a ten foot high fence enclosing the docks. A lorry rumbled past as we pressed back in shadow, but then the road was clear in both directions.

Sakara hissed a soft order and the sergeant with the knapsack crossed the road in a swift crouch. He stopped against the fence, dropping the knapsack to the ground, and bracing himself with his back bent forward and his hands rigid against his knees. Sakara nodded and the second man made his run, using the bowed back as a stepping stone and scrambling neatly over the fence.

Sakara nodded to me and I did it even faster. I had tackled obstacle courses in the marines and I wasn't going to let the old regiment down before a bunch of black soldiers. In fact I had more reasons than one for making a star performance. Sakara came after me, but I reckoned that I was best by a second. The knapsack was thrown over and neatly caught, and then the first man joined us in a slower scramble. The whole operation had taken less than a minute, and when I was sure that we had not been spotted I began to feel that this crazy jaunt just might be successful after all.

We moved deeper into the docks, single file like stealthy Indians. There was plenty of cover in the form of railway trucks, store-buildings and stacked goods, and the sky was clouded black to eliminate all but a scattered handful of stars. Sakara led the way, and I guessed that he must have been born and raised here in Lagos, somewhere close at hand, for he guided us unerringly to the back of Number Two unloading shed. Number Three was to our left, and here I took over, moving to the right and the gap before Number One.

There was a sound over by the railway tracks we had crossed only a minute before, the tread of a nailed boot on a wooden sleeper, and Sakara's hand was upon my shoulder, firmly pressing me down. I crouched silently against the wall, and knew that the three men behind me had done the same. I turned my head cautiously to look to the right and dimly saw the shapes of four Federal soldiers moving quietly between the steel lines. They carried submachine-guns at right angles to their bodies, alert and searching, but not yet aware that there was anything to find. When they had passed on we continued moving, but my heart was doing a few extra beats to the minute.

I turned into the gap between One and Two sheds and then eased down to the next corner to look along the quayside. This corner of the docks was quiet and no ships were being worked.

The berth before Number Two shed was empty, and before Number Three the *African Rose* showed a few lights but was wrapped in silence. There were more armed guards lounging before Number Three, and just round the corner from where I was standing was the stack of twenty-foot timbers that figured prominently in my plans. I turned my head back to signal my trio of sergeants and was just in time to see another of Bumendu's patrols approaching along the quayside between Number One shed and another moored freighter.

I melted back quickly into the darkness, and we all did our huddled freezing act again as the patrol went past. They were walking slowly and making no noise like the previous quartet, but this time they seemed bored with their job and were not searching too closely.

When the way was clear I went forward again, and with Sakara at my side I pointed out the stack of timber. He nodded and signalled to his two colleagues. They slipped past us, crouching low, and moved close along the front of the unloading shed to reach the stack. It formed a shield between themselves and the soldiers further down the quayside, and they deftly drew off one of the heavy three by eight planks from the top of the heap. I sweated as they brought it back into the gap between the sheds but there was no challenge and no alarm.

We checked that it was in fact long enough to span the gap, and then stood it upright against the end wall of Number Two. The roof was our next objective, and while I kept a nervous watch Sakara and his boys did another of their obstacle course acts. This time they made a classic pyramid. Sakara was the base man, number two stood upright on his shoulders, bracing his hands against the wall, and number three scrambled up over their backs until he could straighten up on the middle man's shoulders and stretch up to reach the roof. He hauled himself on top, unslung the coil of rope, and swiftly pulled the rest of us up behind him. We ran up the wall and again the whole operation was very swiftly completed. They were a well-trained team, and I began to feel a little proud of them.

We drew the heavy timber up last, sweating some in our efforts to keep it from scraping over the edge of the roof. When it was aloft we crouched in listening silence for a moment, but so far we were still undetected by the patrols. Finally I nodded, and keeping low we carried the timber across a hundred feet of flat roof until we were stopped by the open gap before Number Three. I inched my head warily over the edge of the roof to look down, but mercifully Bumendu had not thought to post guards at the corners of the building, and if we were silent and lucky the next step was at least possible.

I lashed the rope to one end of the twenty-foot timber, and then we gingerly pushed the tied end out over the gap. The first fifteen feet were easy, but then it began to tilt downwards despite our combined weight. Sakara and I had to stand upright then, taking the weight on the rope and praying that our silhouettes would escape notice for the next vital minute. Inch by inch the timber was thrust out, the need for absolute silence slowing our efforts, and then at last we were able to relax the rope and let the far end lower to rest upon the edge of the roof opposite. The gap was bridged and I was sweating with relief.

I made the first trip across, and the other three quickly followed. The timber bowed a little in the middle, but three by eight was a sturdy thickness and it was nothing alarming. When the crossing was made we again used the rope to draw our makeshift bridge in behind us. It meant that we would have to perform the whole task again to make the return trip, but our work inside the unloading shed would take several hours, and it was too risky to leave the bridge in place where it could be seen by the patrols.

We moved along the roof to the nearest skylight, and then crouched around it. Sakara offered me a big clasp-knife, grinning silently in the darkness, and after two minutes of strong thrusting and twisting with the sharp blade I had the skylight open. We lifted it back with careful hands, and there was no sound from the pitch blackness below. I asked for the torch, and then leaned down into the square hole to switch it on and probe the interior of the long shed. The beam showed everything exactly as I had left it earlier in the day, and there were no guards posted inside. That was a big relief and I switched off the torch and withdrew.

The three sergeants were all grinning, like overgrown ragamuffins out of a Negro folk opera. They worked quickly to lash the rope around the skylight casing, and then dropped it to unfurl in the blackness inside. I went first, lowering myself over the edge and then swinging hand over hand down the rope. It was only a twenty foot drop and my feet touched the concrete floor before I reached the end. I jerked the rope as a signal, and held it taut while the three sergeants slithered down to join me.

My heart was thumping as I switched the torch on again, because now was the perfect time for a trap to be sprung. Nothing happened, and after a moment I spotlit the two separate stacks of cases bearing the name of Alfred Cross & Sons of Bedford, England. We moved towards them and I unpacked the knapsack that one of the sergeants had carried. Each man knew exactly what to do and there was a lot to be done, so we started immediately.

I gave the carpenter's plane to Sakara and he deftly started work on the genuine arms crates, neatly planing off the painted X on each case. The two junior sergeants did the heavy work of carrying the crates back and forth, while I worked with the black paint and the brush to reproduce a neat black X on the cases that were filled with farm tools. It wasn't easy to work with only the one torch, and without giving any audible orders, but we managed reasonably well. There were four hundred crates to be swapped over, but I reckoned that three hours of solid work should see the job done, leaving us just enough time to make our escape before dawn.

It was an unnerving task, the long unloading shed shrouded in total darkness beyond the puny and erratic flickering of the torch beam. From outside we could hear occasional muffled sounds from the guards and the wandering patrols, and inside there was nothing but the slow panting of the two donkey sergeants, or the agonising creak or scrape of a case as it slipped in their hands. About a third of the crates had been shifted when Sakara decided to relieve one of his colleagues, and after that they worked a rota system of sharing the heavy work and taking brief rests with the plane. I was sweating enough already and I stayed with my paintbrush. Another score of crates were moved back and forth and I was painting my seventy-ninth X with careful strokes of the brush, and then the end came. Doors crashed open, lights flashed on, and from three separate points Federal troops rushed forward in an uproar of shouting voices and levelled weapons. And behind them, striding purposefully to demand an explanation, came General Daniel Makefa.

18

Double Bluff

SAKARA was stupid enough to grab for his revolver, and it was his first and last unintelligent move. A single burst from one of the submachine-guns kicked three red holes in his greasy sweat shirt, just above the region of his navel, and tumbled him back ten yards across the concrete floor. The remaining two sergeants quickly put up their hands, and I made it quite obvious to everyone that I was holding nothing more lethal than a paintbrush.

The bright dazzle of the lights had me blinded for a few moments, and it was probably the abrupt and unexpected glare that had confused Sakara into committing suicide. I had to blink several times, and when my vision returned the ring of troops were already breaking to let Makefa through. The two sergeants were seized roughly, but Makefa snapped an order and waved away the soldiers who had started to lay hands on me. Behind him I saw Kamau, grim and poker-faced, and then Major Bumendu with a revolver in his hand. And finally, his black and grey out of place amid the array of army uniforms, I recognised the Police Captain Shabani. The babble from the soldiers died down, and Makefa inspected my handiwork in ominous silence, and then be turned to me with a facial expression like a slab of carved coal and said in an acid voice,

"Very interesting, Major M'Call. It is rather fortunate that Captain Shabani wished to ask you some questions about the white girl who was killed by the rebels. By pure chance it was not until late tonight that he learned that you had returned to Lagos, and when he and Lieutenant Kamau went to your room they found that you were missing.

They searched the Ambassadors Hotel, and then notified me of your absence, and I had the impulse to come here." He glanced coldly at the paintbrush in my hand. "I trust that you have an adequate explanation for this?"

I nodded emphatically. My brain was racing and I was trying hard to think up a good story, but in the meantime I had to do some more fast talking, and bluff better than I had ever bluffed before. I gave him the straight facts about Sallah and Virginia West, filling in all the bits that I had left out previously, and explained exactly how Sallah had arranged to hi-jack the arms from the unguarded trucks that would be taking them out of the docks later in the day. Makefa listened but his face showed no sign of relaxing its black hostility, and even if he believed me there was no sympathy when he said,

"So — to save the life of this girl you have chosen to betray me, and to turn my riles over to the rebels."

"No, General!" I shook my head

firmly at that. "You mistake my intentions entirely. I have no desire to help Nigeria's enemies, but I had no choice but to cooperate with the early stages of their plans. It is not you I intended to betray but Major Sallah. I have been waiting my opportunity and I had hoped that he would accompany me tonight, then I could have raised the alarm and handed him and his three colleagues over to Major Bumendu and his troops once they had trapped themselves in this warehouse. Unfortunately Sallah was too clever for me, he refused to expose himself to any personal risk."

"But you still choose to exchange my rifles for worthless cases of farm tools?"

"I had no choice. Again they would have killed the girl, and I still hoped to trap Major Sallah. Tonight he has played safe, but I am certain that when the attempt is made to seize the trucks carrying the arms then Sallah will be leading the attack. He expects the trucks to be unguarded, and he will be taken completely by surprise if they are loaded with your Federal troops. This was my plan, but for the sake of the girl I could not risk informing you until the last minute. If tonight's work had been successful then I would have earned Sallah's trust, and increased our chances of success."

Makefa said bluntly, "You would also have increased the rebels' chances of acquiring ten thousand brand-new automatic rifles at the expense of my Government. Your explanations are feeble, Major M'Call, and even if you are telling the truth then I do not estimate that the life of one girl and the capture of one rebel officer is worth the risk."

It was time to play my only two aces and I slapped them down boldly, facing Makefa directly in the eyes.

"General, you're wrong. This particular major and this particular girl are worth any amount of risk. Cast your mind back to the murder of Sir Stanley

Okuwa. You told me once that Nigeria faces a wave of bloodshed at the end of the fast of Ramadan unless the Premier's killers are brought to justice. Major Sallah was the rebel officer who directed the massacre at the villa, and it was he personally who put a pistol to Okuwa's head and blew out his brains. And the girl is a living witness to that crime."

Makefa stared at me with doubting eyes, but suddenly all the other uncompromising faces ringed around me were taking a sharper interest. The black peaked cap and grey shirt of Captain Shabani pushed forward between Kamau and Bumendu and the policeman said tersely,

"Then Virginia West *was* the white teacher who accompanied John Sikuvu to the Premier's garden party?"

I nodded, and told him exactly what Virginia had told me. They were all listening now, and I made the most of my opportunity to swing them on to my side, diverting their frigid anger from myself towards Sallah. Okuwa had been a popular man, and I spared no detail of his death as I knew it. I finished again on the stark theme of Ramadan, and the threat of a Moslem war of reprisal that could follow. Shabani interrupted me by demanding curtly,

"Why did you not tell me this before, Major M'Call? I had reasons to believe that this girl might have survived the massacre at the garden party, but when I questioned you, you pretended that you knew nothing about her."

"But I didn't know anything, not at that time. She came back later and told me the full story."

"Then why did you not bring her direct to me?"

"She was afraid of you." I didn't want to go too deeply into that and hurried on. "She asked me to take her to the British High Commission, and as I knew that the High Commissioner would undoubtedly call you to hear her story I didn't think that there would be any harm. That was when we were grabbed by the rebels, and since then she's been held a prisoner by Major Sallah."

"And Sallah does not know that she is a witness against him?"

Shabani was giving me a very doubting look indeed, one that was worthy of any policeman in the world, but this time I could answer with absolute honesty.

"No, Sallah isn't aware of that, and I keep praying that he won't find out."

Shabani was only warming up with the questions, but Makefa had tired of relinquishing the limelight. The army had preference over the police force and the General broke into the cross examination with some more questions of his own.

"Major M'Call, your story has a possible ring of truth, but if it is true then there is one very definite flaw. Why did you not explain everything to me immediately after your return from Kaduna. We could have then worked together to trap this Major

Sallah and to release the girl. Surely this should have been the obvious procedure, and a much more certain one than your own idiotic tricks here tonight?"

That was an awkward one, but remembering Virginia's story had given me a merciful flash of inspiration and I said quickly,

"Normally I would agree, General, but not in this case. I had to work alone because I have reason to believe that there is a traitor in your confidence."

Makefa was rattled, his certainty shaken for the second time. He stared at me for a moment and I didn't flinch, and then he said slowly,

"I think you should explain that, Major M'Call."

I said simply, "I'm referring to a Government Minister whom I understand is a close friend of yours, a Chief Malundi. He was also at the Premier's garden party when Sallah and his troops made their attack, and Malundi was also able to escape with his life — either that or Sallah *allowed* him to get away." I was gambling in the dark now but it was too late to draw back, and I had to make it sound as though my suspicions were all on Malundi and not on Makefa himself.

I went on, "The important fact is that Malundi was also a witness to what happened that day, but obviously he did not inform you. Otherwise you would not have remained ignorant of Okuwa's fate for two whole days. Therefore I can only assume that he is a traitor."

There were many ears straining now, Kamau, Bumendu, and practically a whole platoon of soldiery. For a second I had turned the tables and put Makefa on the spot, but it didn't last. The General said grimly,

"I can assure you that Chief Malundi is loyal. He did inform me personally of what had happened, but it was a political necessity to keep Sir Stanley Okuwa's death uncertain until the *start* of the fast of Ramadan. The danger of an outbreak of Moslem violence was even greater the two days before the fast began than it will be when the fast ends."

It was a good answer, and it didn't matter that I was as unsure of his motives as he was of mine. The listeners were all impressed, and I had an intuitive feeling that Makefa had no desire to go any deeper into that particular argument. Already I had revealed enough. Perhaps there were other skeletons in his cupboard that I didn't know about, but he didn't know how much I knew and he was taking no chances. He changed the subject and asked,

"Where is Sallah holding the girl now?"

"I don't know." I risked a wry smile and added, "If I did I could have tried something other than these idiotic tricks you have interrupted."

Makefa didn't smile, instead he turned to gaze hard at Sallah's two sergeants, who were still held fast and helpless by the toughest of his troops. He said grimly,

"Do these men know?"

I knew what he intended and my stomach felt faintly squeamish. They were good men, even if they were on the wrong side, but the world has no justice for the losers. I remembered Virginia, so young and so vulnerable, and then answered, "I'm certain that they must know."

"Then they will tell us," Makefa decided.

★ ★ ★

The selected victim lasted fifteen minutes before the Federal soldiers succeeded in beating the truth out of him. They worked unscientifically, using fists and boots and rifle butts, and splashing an unnecessary amount of blood over the grey concrete floor, but they achieved results. My former ally talked through a broken mouth, and Major Bumendu approached Makefa to report.

The squad of troops that Sallah commanded was encamped in dense jungle some twenty-five miles to the northeast, but Sallah himself had made his headquarters in a small village only just outside of Lagos where his uncle was the headman. And Virginia was with Sallah at the village.

Kamau said swiftly that he knew the village.

Makefa smiled at him, a sudden fatherly smile.

"Then you will lead the way, Lieutenant. And you, Major M'Call, will accompany us. It will be an excellent opportunity to test some of the new armoured cars supplied by your company. We will raid the village first to capture this Major Sallah, and then the cars can be sent north-east to destroy his rebel troops."

He started to turn briskly away, but I knew that I couldn't let him go charging into that native village in a cloud of noise and dust merely to display his new toys. I stopped him and said earnestly,

"General, if you move in with force then Sallah will almost certainly see you coming. He'll kill the girl and escape into the jungle."

He stared at me for a moment, and then nodded his head.

"Perhaps you are right, but what do you suggest?"

I drew a deep breath, praying that I really was back in favour, and then said,

"Give me two men and let me go in first. Sallah is expecting his three sergeants to return in their Land-Rover before dawn, and if we use their vehicle then we stand a good chance of taking him by surprise. We can disarm him and hold him until your main force arrives."

Makefa was hesitant, he didn't really trust me but he knew that what I suggested made sense. He frowned for a long moment, and then made his decision and turned to Kamau.

"Lieutenant, pick another capable man to go with Major M'Call, and you will be in command of the Land-Rover."

19

Desperate Move

MAKEFA was reluctant to
trust me with a gun, but
after some argument I was
allowed to borrow Kamau's revolver.
Kamau and the stocky corporal he had
chosen to make the third man had
both armed themselves with Stirling
submachine-guns. They stripped off
their uniforms and donned the greasy
stevedore's rags that had been worn
by Sallah's two surviving sergeants,
but then we were delayed for an
hour while Makefa organised his own
forces. He was determined to make
an armoured car charge close behind
us, and not until he was ready
were we allowed to lead off in the
Land-Rover.

Kamau took the wheel with his

corporal beside him, their submachine-guns pushed down out of sight behind their feet. I sat in the back with the revolver on the seat beside me. Makefa promised us a ten minute start and reminded us that he wanted Sallah alive, and then he saluted and stepped back. Kamau answered the salute, and then slammed in the clutch and we were away.

The final arrangements had been made at the army camp, and so we had only to cut back through the outskirts of Lagos, by-passing the main island city to reach the jungle road leading east to the village. Kamau explained that it was merely an open market place surrounded by some three score of mud huts about ten miles distant.

The road was narrow, with dense jungle pressing in and overhanging from each side, and the grey light of dawn was advancing fast. There was a damp, swampy smell coming out of the forest, mixed with the wild aroma of flowers, and filtered by a layer of dust. The

Land-Rover was jolting and bouncing as Kamau kept his foot flat down, and he seemed determined to get there as quickly as possible and make a clean sweep before Makefa could arrive. A blue and red lizard flashed out of the road and into the undergrowth and very narrowly escaped being pulped beneath our wheels. The monkeys chattered noisily at our intrusion, and at any moment I expect that an extra large bump would send us crashing after the lizard. After eight miles had registered on the speedometer clock Kamau braked and then swung the Land-Rover down an even narrower track. He didn't take his eyes from the road, but he turned his head an inch to inform me that the village was less than half a mile ahead. It was now or never and regretfully I touched his own revolver to the back of his neck.

"Then this is where you stop, Lieutenant. I'm sorry, but from here I'm taking the Land-Rover in alone."

Kamau was startled. He looked

round, swerved, and lost a small element of control. The Land-Rover almost turned into the jungle and crunched its nearside wheels through a mass of fern and greenery before he could bring it to a skidding halt back in the centre of the road. He knocked it out of gear and then shifted round to face me with a look of bitter contempt on his face.

"So, Major, you do intend to betray us after all!"

I shook my head. "No, Lieutenant. But Sallah will hear the Land-Rover approach. He's smart enough to stay out of sight until he's sure of what is happening, and the moment he realises that it is not his own three men returning he will still have time to kill the girl and escape into the jungle. You said that there were sixty huts, remember, and it will take several minutes to find which one he is using. A few minutes is all that Sallah will need, and once he gets under cover an army would never find him in this stuff."

Kamau noted the density of the jungle and accepted my point, but he wasn't wholly convinced. He said curtly,

"General Makefa will not approve of this change of plans."

I knew all about that. Makefa would have realised that I was more interested in saving Virginia than ensuring that Sallah didn't make his escape, and that was why I hadn't suggested to him that I should go in entirely alone. Now I had to risk the general's wrath again but it was the only way. To Kamau I put it a little differently.

"I didn't realise until now how easy it will still be for Sallah to escape. But I appreciate that you cannot accept a change in your orders, and that is why I am taking full responsibility. I'll go in first and I should be able to get close to Sallah. He'll want to know what's happened. Then I'm expecting close support from you, Lieutenant. You said that the village is less than half a mile, which means that if you and the Corporal run fast then you'll be only a matter of minutes behind me."

Kamau said grimly, "We shall be close behind you, Major. You may depend on that."

I smiled. "I am depending upon it, Lieutenant, and I'm positive that you won't fail me."

Kamau wasn't appeased, but he made no more protest when I ordered him to get out into the road. The corporal gave me a dark look but he followed the example of his officer, and when they were both standing well back I wriggled through into the front seat behind the wheel. The engine was still running and I put my foot on the clutch and rammed in the second gear. Then I reached down and fished out the two submachine-guns.

"You'll need these," I said, and I tossed them one each. Then I let my foot off the clutch and stamped on the accelerator, and the Land-Rover scooted forward in a flurry of dust.

I crashed into third and then looked briefly back to see that both men had started to run after me. Kamau could have shot me in the back before I got out of range but I had gambled that he wouldn't, and I knew that I could rely upon him to follow me just as fast as his feet could carry him. I turned away then and concentrated on getting a couple of minutes start.

The Land-Rover was jumping about in an agony of suffering springs, but I managed to hold it with one hand while I snapped the safety on Kamau's revolver and then pushed it down the back of my pants close against my spine. There it would be out of sight and covered by my jacket, and if Sallah came close enough to search me then at least I would have him within arms reach. I put both hands on the wheel again and then drove flat out until suddenly the jungle cleared away on each side and was shooting into the middle of the promised collection of mud huts.

A flight of skinny chickens fluttered up squawking from beneath my wheels as I braked hard in the centre of the village, and an outraged dog set up a clamour of barking. A few women in brightly coloured turbans and mammy cloths stared at me from between the huts where they had started to light the morning cooking fires, and a tame monkey took fright and went scrambling back into the surrounding palm trees. I shut off the engine and then climbed out into what was presumably the empty market clearing, and then three Negroes wearing khaki shorts and grubby vests suddenly rushed at me from behind one of the huts, all of them pointing rifle barrels at my middle.

I hadn't calculated that Sallah would have kept a few of his troops close as a bodyguard, or perhaps he needed them to reinforce Sakara and the other two sergeants for the hijacking job. However, they were here and I quickly put up my hands. They had recognised the Land-Rover but they had not recognised me, and they considered that a reasonable excuse to be suspicious and unfriendly. They surrounded me and said nothing, but the noise of my arrival had caused the villagers to emerge from their huts and begin to jabber curiously. The men were mostly wearing trousers and vests, or trousers and scraps of shirts, but one older man came towards me wearing a white *agbada* robe. There was intricate black embroidery around the neck and down the front, and I guessed that this must be the headman. He was a too regal figure for a village as small as this one, but I noticed that his calloused feet were bare. I assumed that he could speak English and said swiftly,

"Take me to Major Sallah, quickly! Our plans have gone wrong.

He hesitated, glancing back along the track. Then he nodded and turned away without speaking. I moved boldly past the threatening rifles and followed him between two of the straw and mud huts. I could hear the three armed soldiers padding at my heels but I didn't look round.

A Negro woman moved hastily out of our way, grabbing up a naked child who had stopped to gaze up at me with wondering eyes. The dog barked again and a late cockerel suddenly realised that it had missed the dawn. I felt that damned revolver slip down even further along my spine, but I couldn't change step or do anything about it. I could only visualise myself looking a right fool if it slipped right through and fell down my leg. I began to sweat, an all too frequent habit over the past few days, and then abruptly Sallah appeared in the doorway to the next hut.

He was still wearing his dark blue suit with the slim tie, but his polite smile was missing from his face. Instead he wore a tight-lipped expression of stony surprise, and he looked as though this time he was only waiting for the right moment to use the revolver in his hand. He said harshly,

"Major M'Call, what has happened?"

"It's all gone wrong," I told him obscurely. "The whole thing is a complete bloody mess. We'd better go inside and I can explain."

He eyed me as he might have done a black mamba, and then he snapped an order to his bodyguard. They hurried away and I guessed that they were going to keep watch on the track entering the village, and I hoped that Kamau was as good as he wanted to be. Then Sallah backed up into the hut and I ducked my head below the straw thatch and followed him inside.

The hut smelled dankly of bare earth, and a lizard scuttled somewhere above our heads. It was dark inside and I knew that Sallah's eyes must be more accustomed to the gloom than mine. I had separated him from his men but he still had the edge. I glanced around the interior and picked out a blur of white moving up from the floor against the far wall, and then Virginia's voice said thankfully,

"Mike! Mike, it is you! What's happening?"

The white blur was the white blouse she was wearing, and I was so relieved that she was alive that I couldn't answer. Sallah had moved so that he was safe from both of us and he ordered tartly,

"Be quiet, Miss West. I will ask the questions."

I smiled in her direction and said quietly,

"It's all right, Virgin. Stay where you are." Then I looked back to Sallah and changed my tone.

"The arms switch didn't work out, you've probably guessed that by now. Makefa caught us inside the warehouse, and I was the only one to get away. Sakara is dead and your other two friends are prisoners. I came here to warn you as quickly as I could."

"How did you know that you would find me here?"

"Because one of your sergeants talked and I was there to hear it. I didn't make my break until afterwards."

I was trying to get closer as I talked but he was having none of that. He motioned me back with the revolver and said flatly,

"My men would not betray me."

I said just as flatly, "Makefa's soldiers worked on him with their rifle butts. They broke his arm, a couple of ribs, his nose, and bashed out most of his teeth. Then he betrayed you."

My own eyes were adjusting to the gloom and I could see that his expression had not changed. His thick lips barely parted as he asked,

"And why should you come here to warn me? We have no love for each other, Major M'Call, and I cannot believe that you have any sincere concern for my continued good health."

I said bluntly, "I haven't. But I have

got a concern for the girl. I couldn't get the arms for you, but at least I'm giving you a chance to save your skin. If you have any honour as an officer you will recognise that and spare me the girl."

As I spoke I half-turned to gesture with my left hand towards Virginia, while my right hand moved tentatively towards the revolver that lay flat against my spine. Sallah's eyes were sharper than I had realised and he snapped swiftly,

"Keep your hands where I can see them. If they move out of my sight I will shoot you instantly."

I brought my hands back into view and said earnestly,

"But, Major Sallah, you don't understand — "

"The point is that I do understand, Major M'Call. You are one of the most fluent liars that I have ever met. You interpret your own motives to please whoever happens to be listening. I cannot accept anything that you say, and it would not surprise me if you have already led Makefa and his soldiers directly to this village."

"You're wrong," I said firmly. "But Makefa will be arriving in less than ten minutes, you can take that as gospel. He doesn't need me to lead him. You still have a chance to escape, but only if — "

I didn't finish because in that moment three rifles and two submachine-guns opened up a simultaneous burst of frantic firing on the edge of the village. The chickens began a clamour of fresh squawking, the dogs howled in terror, and women and children screamed in frenzy. The confusion was abrupt and deafening, and I knew that Lieutenant Kamau and his corporal had arrived. Sallah swung sharply to face the sound and for a split second his revolver was no longer trained on my belly. I knew that it was the last shadow of a chance that I would ever get in this world, and in the same moment I jumped him.

He fired automatically, but I was veering right and the bullet scorched a hot path beside my left ribs without tearing anything more solid than my jacket. My flying leap would have carried me right past him if I had not hooked my left arm savagely around his throat, and as he staggered back with me I swung my own body neatly behind him. I dragged him down in a heap and as we fell I reached around him with my right hand to grab at his own right which held the gun. He had the sense to know that if another bullet blasted out of the barrel then the odds were that it would lodge in his own gut rather than mine and he chose to let the revolver fall. Then we were rolling and squirming desperately over the hard earth floor.

I was dimly aware that the submachine-guns were still blazing away somewhere outside, but I had too much on my own mind to worry about Kamau's problems. I had the single arm lock on Sallah's throat, but now that he had both hands free it didn't last for long. We performed about three complete rolls across the floor and the act ended with Sallah underneath and forcing himself on to his hands and knees. He made one furious effort to lift us both upright, and then his hands clamped on my left wrist and shoulder and he arched his back to throw me heavily across the hut. I sprawled with a hefty crash on one shoulder, and then twisted round gasping and spitting dirt to meet his next attack. Fortunately he chose to rush in again rather than retrieve his gun and I kicked out to land a lucky boot squarely in his groin.

He howled with agony and crashed back against the side of the hut, bringing down a shower of straw, lizards, and scraps of dry mud as the roof quivered under the impact, and by the time he had recovered I had got back to my feet. He came at me again, but my own revolver was still tucked against my spine, and had dealt me a painful mass of bruises in the general rough and tumble to prove it. I stood my ground and succeeded in pulling it free, and as Sallah closed in I cracked him a merciless wallop across the side of the head with the barrel. He went spinning sideways and fell.

I was only just in time, for a ghost-like figure had just appeared to fill the hut doorway. I recognised the headsman in his long white *agbada* robe, and I didn't care much for the savage expression on his face, nor the sharp-pointed native spear which he had obviously considered a fitting ornament for my back. I cocked the revolver and said harshly,

"Drop it. Now!"

He sulked, but then tossed the spear into a corner of the hut. Outside the shooting had stopped, and I could hear Kamau's voice raised on an ordering note of triumph, and it seemed as good a time as any to go out there and find out what was happening. I gestured to Sallah and told the headman to drag him out into the open, and sullenly the man obeyed. Virginia was suddenly pressing close beside me, and I put my free arm around her and gave her a warming squeeze. I smiled at her, kissed her lightly on the nose, and said softly,

"It's over, Virgin. Come on out and see the sunshine."

Her steps faltered a little uncertainly, but together we emerged from the hut. Sallah was lying on the ground, blinking his eyes and beginning to stir again, and his uncle the headman was kneeling over him. The whole village seemed to have gathered around us with the men at the fore, and I noticed with some renewed apprehension that most of the menfolk had quietly armed themselves with knives and more spears. Then Kamau and his corporal appeared from between two of the huts, both alive and smiling and looking well pleased with themselves. They had their submachine-guns levelled and in front of them marched two of Sallah's soldiers with their hands clasped on top of their heads. Kamau saluted me briskly, and explained that the third soldier had been shot dead. The two prisoners had promptly thrown their guns away when the odds had been made even.

Sallah recovered in time to get the gist of the story and he glared at his crestfallen allies with a look of disgust. Then he got unsteadily to his feet, ignoring the blood that was trickling down the side of his dark face, and began to speak swiftly to his uncle. Before he could finish Kamau stepped in with a threatening movement of his submachine-gun and said sharply,

"Stop that! Or I kill you now."

The tension was building up again and I was conscious of the glowering faces of the villagers. The headman was like a shrouded statue, his face frigid, but his eyes flickering to read the signs as he calculated over Sallah's suggestion. Kamau and his corporal half-turned to face the village and their faces were tense. I tasted my dry lips and asked,

"What's happening?"

Kamau said grimly,

"Major Sallah has asked the headman to turn his spearmen against us."

I stared at the watching black faces. Spears against submachine-guns would be madness, but we were encircled and three accurate spears in the back would be enough if they were incensed enough to try. The headman looked undecided and I pointed my revolver at him to let him know that he would most certainly be among the dead. Virginia pressed close beside me, but I didn't dare take my eyes from the headman's face to look at her. And then that late-rising cock crowed again on the edge of the village, like a noisy herald. There was a roar of engines, and amid a cloud of dust and with a charging flourish, Makefa's armoured cars swept out of the jungle and snarled to a stop in the centre of the village. The headman looked around sharply, and then bowed his head in defeat. He offered a few apologetic words to Kamau and the young lieutenant smiled scornfully. Then Kamau lowered his submachine-gun and turned to me, still smiling, to translate.

"The headman asks me to tell the General that he is very sorry if his poor village has caused any trouble. He says that he did not know that his unworthy nephew was a rebel."

20

I DIDN'T catch that noon plane, but I was aboard the next flight that left twenty-four hours later. By then Virginia had told everything she knew and signed statements for both Makefa and Shabani, and she accompanied me aboard. Kamau came to see us off, and this time I don't think he was under orders. I shook his hand in a warm farewell. I had begun to like him even though I wasn't sorry to be saying good-bye. Then I rejoined Virginia inside the waiting VC10, glad to escape from the blistering sunlight. Ten minutes later we were smoothly airborne. Lagos airfield had vanished, Nigeria was receding fast at approximately nine miles per minute, and we had B.O.A.C. to take care of us.

An air hostess came round, with a

smile for everybody and a selection of reading material to while away the flight time. I accepted a Daily Mirror in order to catch up on my favourite comic strips, but Virginia chose the New Nigerian. She rustled the pages for a few minutes and then said in a puzzled voice,

"Mike, there's not a word in here about the capture of Major Sallah. No mention at all."

I stopped admiring Garth's latest half-naked girl-friend and looked towards her.

"Did you expect that there would be?"

"Of course I did. I thought it would be headline news. After all, he is Sir Stanley Okuwa's murderer. If the Premier's followers don't know that Sallah has been captured and brought to justice then there's still nothing to stop an outbreak of Moslem violence at the end of Ramadan."

I said, "Precisely, and that's why it's most likely that Makefa will have Sallah quietly executed in some dark corner of a prison courtyard. He doesn't want any publicity."

She was staring at me, her expression bewildered.

"But we handed Sallah over for a public trial, to avert the possibility of bloodshed."

I put my hand on her arm and tried hard to explain.

"Virgin, you have to stop thinking in terms of humanitarian ideals, and start thinking in terms of political expediency; at least when you're dealing with politicians and men of power. There are a few exceptions, but if you base your thinking on that factor then your calculations will be right more often than they're wrong. In this case Makefa now has the arms and the armoured cars he needs to crush the army rebellion in Kaduna. He'll have that under control and Major-General Karagwe and his Revolutionary Council all neatly executed long before the end of Ramadan. Then if the Moslems are foolish enough to start a delayed uprising Makefa has his hands free to deal with them also, and a perfect excuse to purge any of the Moslem leaders strong enough to oppose him. After that General Daniel Makefa is all set for a long rule as Nigeria's supreme strongman, with the Federal Government nicely in his pocket, and that is what General Daniel Makefa wants. That's why he'll hush up Sallah's arrest if he possibly can, and that's why you're on this plane instead of being detained in Lagos as a witness to the trial. If Makefa can arrange things his way Sallah won't get a trial — just a bullet."

"But — but Lieutenant Kamau knows about Sallah, and that Major Bumendu. They can't all be covering up."

"No, but Kamau wants to lead the charge into Kaduna. Makefa will let him, and Bumendu will probably be sent in with the first attack as well. If Makefa is lucky then both Kamau and Bumendu will be killed. They'll be buried with full military honours and Makefa will shed crocodile tears at their heroes funeral. It's a very old routine."

"But the Police Captain — Shabani. He knows too!"

"Shabani can have an accident, or be bought."

Her face was still bewildered, but now there was a kind of pale horror there as well. She said helplessly,

"Then Makefa will get away with it?"

"For a while maybe, but few men survive for long in African politics. Somewhere along the line there'll be another Daniel Makefa, just like our Daniel Makefa but under another name. And our Daniel Makefa will fall and vanish. His reign can only be brief. The signs all point to the Ibo tribes in Biafra forming a breakaway state from the Federation somewhere in the not-too-distant future. Then there'll be civil war and a few million Nigerians will get killed. That could well be Makefa's downfall, always assuming that he lasts that long. There's always blood at a birth, and the whole continent of Africa is being reborn."

Virginia was silent for a moment, and then she said bitterly,

"You had all this worked out beforehand, didn't you? And yet you still handed Sallah over to Makefa without any argument."

I said simply, "Sallah was a cold-blooded murderer. He deserves all he'll get. And I had no choice but to hand him over to Makefa. He was our ticket out."

She looked at me and there was a hopeless mist over her lilac-blue eyes. She said in a low voice,

"You're a bastard, M'Call."

It was the first time that I had ever heard her use a swear word, but it didn't offend me. I never allowed myself to be offended by the truth. I said quietly,

"That's quite right. I never knew

my father, my mother brought me up alone. Perhaps being a literal bastard does help to make me one in both senses of the word. I don't really know."

She said nothing, but some strange peak of emotion had been reached within her, like a late reaction to all the bravery she had shown during the past few days. Her mouth didn't tremble but her eyes were crying. I put my hand on her arm and said very softly, "It's all right, Virgin, go ahead and weep. Weep for our whole sorry, stupid, muddled and suicidal world. Perhaps your tears will do some good. Mine didn't, and I'm too old to have any left."

And so she wept, silently and inwardly, and after a minute I called the air hostess and ordered two double shots of Seagram's V.O. with one small bottle of dry ginger ale. They didn't have any Seagram's and so I had to settle for Scotch.

A FOOT IN THE GRAVE
Bruce Marshall

About to be imprisoned and tortured in Buenos Aires, John Smith escapes, only to become involved in an aeroplane hijacking.

DEAD TROUBLE
Martin Carroll

Trespassing brought Jennifer Denning more than she bargained for. She was totally unprepared for the violence which was to lie in her path.

HOURS TO KILL
Ursula Curtiss

Margaret went to New Mexico to look after her sick sister's rented house and felt a sharp edge of fear when the absent landlady arrived.